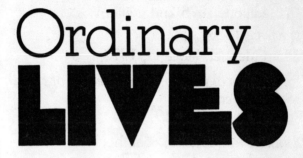

Ordinary
LIVES

Other Titles by Irving Kenneth Zola

Origins of Crime, collaborator
(Columbia University Press, New York, 1959)

Poverty & Health, coeditor
(Harvard University Press, Cambridge, 1969
  1st edition, 1975 2nd edition)

De Medische Macht
(Boom Meppel, Holland, 1973)

*Organizational Issues in the Delivery of Health
  Services*, coeditor
(Prodist, New York, 1974)

Disabling Professions, coauthor
(Marion Boyars, U.K., 1977)

Missing Pieces
(Temple University Press, Philadelphia, 1982)

Independent Living in America, coeditor
(Jossey-Bass, California, 1982)

Ordinary
LIVES

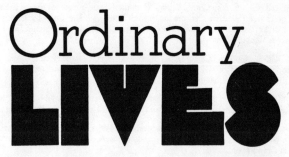

Voices of disability & disease

Edited by Irving Kenneth Zola

Apple-wood Books
Cambridge/Watertown
1982

Ordinary Lives: Voices of Disability and Disease
Edited by Irving Kenneth Zola
Copyright © 1982 Apple-wood Books, Inc.
ISBN: 0-918222-36-2 (hardcover)

We gratefully acknowledge the following permissions:

CHRISTY BROWN: From *My Left Foot: The Story of Christy Brown* by Christy Brown. Copyright © 1954, 1955 by Christy Brown. Reprinted by permission of Simon & Schuster, a Division of Gulf & Western Corporation. From *Down All The Days* by Christy Brown. Copyright © 1970 by Christy Brown. Reprinted with permission of Stein and Day Publishers and Secker & Warburg Ltd

ERIC HODGINS: "God and Carrot Juice" in *Episode: Report on the Accident Inside My Skull* by Eric Hodgins. Copyright © 1963 by Eric Hodgins (New York: Atheneum, 1964). Reprinted with the permission of Atheneum Publishers.

HAROLD KRENTS: From *To Race the Wind* by Harold Krents. Copyright © 1972 by Harold Krents. Reprinted by permission of Hawthorn Properties (Elsevier-Dutton Publishing Co., Inc.)

MARTHA WEINMAN LEAR: From *Heartsounds* by Martha Weinman Lear. Copyright 1980 by Martha Weinman Lear. Reprinted by permission of Simon and Schuster, A Division of Gulf & Western Corporation.

VED MEHTA: From *Face to Face* by Ved Mehta. Copyright © 1957 by Ved Mehta. Reprinted by permission of Harold Ober Associates Incorporated.

VASSAR MILLER: "Spastics" is reprinted from *If I Could Sleep Deeply Enough, Poems by Vassar Miller.* Copyright © 1968, 1972, 1973, 1974 by Vassar Miller. With permission of the publisher, Liveright Publishing Corporation.

FLANNERY O'CONNOR: "Good Country People" is from *A Good Man is Hard to Find and Other Stories* by Flannery O'Connor. Copyright © 1955, by Flannery O'Connor. Reprinted by permission of Harcourt Brace Jovanich, Inc.

ANDREW POTOK: From *Ordinary Daylight* by Andrew Potok. Copyright © 1980 by Andrew Potok. Reprinted by permission of Holt, Rinehart and Winston, Publishers.

ADRIENNE RICH: "A Woman Dead in Her Forties" is reprinted from *The Dream of a Common Language, Poems 1974-1977,* by Adrienne Rich. Copyright © 1978 by W.W. Norton & Company, Inc. By permission of the author and the publisher, W.W. Norton & Company, Inc.

BETTY ROLLIN: Chapter 18 (pp. 151-167) in *First, You Cry* by Betty Rollin (J.B. Lippincott Co.) Copyright © 1976 by Betty Rollin. Reprinted by permission of Harper & Row, Publishers, Inc.

ALEXANDER SOLZHENITSYN: From *Cancer Ward* by Alexander Solzhenitsyn, translated by Nicholas Bethell and David Burg. © 1968 by Alexander Solzhenitsyn. English translation © 1968, 1969 by The Bodley Head Ltd. Reprinted by permission of Farrar, Straus and Giroux, Inc. and The Bodley Head Ltd.

FRANCES WARFIELD: A selection from *Cotton in My Ears* by Frances Warfield. Copyright 1948 by Frances Warfield Hackett. Copyright 1948 by The Curtis Publishing Company. Used by permission of Viking Penguin Inc.

IRVING KENNETH ZOLA: "With Heironymous Bosch in India" was originally published in *Missing Pieces* by Irving Kenneth Zola. Copyright © 1982 by Irving Kenneth Zola. Reprinted by permission of Temple University Press. "And the Children Shall Lead Us" originally appeared in *Disabled USA*.

To Judy, who has given voice to so many others.

CONTENTS

Introduction   11

Frontispiece   17
  "Spastics" by Vassar Miller

I
  From *Cotton in my Ears* by Frances Warfield   21
  "And The Children Shall Lead Us"
  by Irving Kenneth Zola   34
  From *My Left Foot* by Christy Brown   38
  From *The Long Walk Home* by Leonard Kriegel   46
  From *Ordinary Daylight* by Andrew Potok   53
  From *Heartsounds* by Martha Weinman Lear   62

II
  From *The Long Walk Home* by Leonard Kriegel   71
  From *Face to Face* by Ved Mehta   84
  From *To Race the Wind* by Harold Krents   99
  "With Heironymous Bosch in India"
  by Irving Kenneth Zola   105
  From *First, You Cry* by Betty Rollin   113
  From *Episode* by Eric Hodgins   128

III
  From *Down all the Days* by Christy Brown   137
  From *To Race the Wind* by Harold Krents   147
  From *The Long Walk Home* by Leonard Kriegel   154
  "Good Country People" by Flannery O'Connor   161
  From *Cancer Ward* by Alexander Solzhenitsyn   188
  From *Ordinary Daylight* by Andrew Potok   198
  From *Heartsounds* by Martha Weinman Lear   204
  "Tell Me, Tell Me" by Irving Kenneth Zola   208

Backpiece   217
  "A Woman Dead in Her Forties" by Adrienne Rich

Irving Kenneth Zola

Introduction

I began writing this introduction in 1981, a year officially designated by the United Nations as the International Year of the Disabled. It certainly has been a year, or really two, in which people with disabilities and chronic diseases have been featured in novels, plays, and movies. I suppose that's a good thing. Although frankly, I'm ambivalent. Part of my uncertainty comes from the messages of too many of these stories. They seem to be, all too often, tales of superhuman heroism and courage. The stories bring up in me, and I think in my fellow "crips," some of the same isolation we feel in the TV telethons where money is raised for "those poor unfortunates."

For like it or not, in high technology America few die anymore of old age. Most of us will instead be afflicted with some set of initials—an MCI, a CVA, or even CA. The fund-raising telethons, the TV shows, the movies each blocks out that reality. I think it *is* important that the public learn that just because someone has had polio, or a stroke, suffers from multiple sclerosis or cancer, has had a heart attack or lost the use of his or her arms and legs, she or he can still be a mother, father, lover, doctor, writer, and accomplish great deeds. But the *who* and the *how* of these depictions is often quite unreal.

There is another false note to the current spate of stories. The climax almost always seems to be centered around some specific obstacle the person overcame or some special goal achieved. And when this happens, lifelong 'health' and 'happiness' are over the next hill. I like happy endings and once-and-for-all settlement of basic issues; but life, certainly for those of us with a chronic disease or disability, is not like that. In fact it's just the opposite. It is in the nature of a chronic disability or chronic disease that it essentially lasts forever. Depressing but true. And though it need not dominate or limit our lives, dealing with it is a continuing struggle—not a battle to be won once and for all.

People in the Western world have great difficulty accepting such realities. We continually deny that we may get old, sick, disabled, and die. We think of those things as happening to someone else. And in all those denials we deplete ourselves of the very resources to deal with our own inevitable fallibility. And as long as we deny such vulnerability in ourselves, we will never be able to accept the disease and disability in others.

I put together this anthology in order to find another way to bridge this gap. The title of this collection is *Ordinary Lives: Voices of Disability and Disease*. And that is what these selections are about. While in each, the issue of a person's disease or disability is prominent, the stories are not primarily about coping or overcoming. They are about all the emotional issues of daily living—the times we get angry at events out of our control, our gropings at dating and sex, our frustrations when we find ourselves dependent on someone else, our comings, our goings, our loves and our hatreds. Sometimes we win, sometimes we lose. Sometimes you may think we are just the kind of person you'd like to have for a friend, and sometimes you would rather have nothing to do with us.

I make no claim, as other people with a disability might, that the essence of what I experience is inherently incommunicable to the able-bodied world. I do not believe that there is anything in the nature of having a disease or disability that makes it unsharable or even untellable. It is rather society's denial and the resulting distancing which mutes the vocabulary of experience. With such alienation, it is simply that at this moment those of us who have lived with a disability are often in a better position to write about what it is like. Thus, the stories, tales, and vignettes collected in this book are all by someone who has intimately experienced disease or disability.

Of course, most people are born into the world of the able-bodied. We only become disabled or learn we are physically different later. We are socialized into the same world as everyone else, with many of the same expectations as well as prejudices. Thus having a disability or disease, or living with someone who has, does not automatically qualify us either to be an expert witness or a writer. For this anthology I have chosen authors who, while writing about disease and disability, are also writing about the human condition.

The sources of my selections are diverse and include autobiographies, essays, novels, short stories, and poetry. I hope that whatever else they are, these are good stories—ones that make you laugh, or cry, or think about what you've read. As for more detail, I plead the caution of Flannery O'Connor:

". . . A story is a way to say something that can't be said any other way, and it takes every word in the story to say what the meaning is. You tell a story because a statement would be inadequate. When anybody asks what a story is about, the only proper thing is to tell him to read the story."

This anthology would not have existed but for my publisher and editor, Phil Zuckerman of Apple-wood Books. Nearly three years ago he broached the idea of putting together 'something' about disability. First he looked around for suitable material and then he tried to solicit manuscripts. Nothing much came of it. We believed there was good writing out there, but we did not know how to get at it. Most of all, it was apparent that someone would have to devote 'serious energy' to the pursuit. And so it was about two years ago that I became 'the someone.'

All too often the search proved frustrating. I would find a great book, but it would be unexcerptable. I would hear of a well-known writer with a disability, but she or he had written essays about his/her issues, not stories describing his/her experiences. I thought the progress was slow, but Phil was patient. If not this fall, then next spring...if not this winter, then next summer. And gradually it began to come together.

Soon friends and relatives, colleagues and librarians were calling in their suggestions. At times it felt as if I had an army of research assistants. But one person, more than any other, was my best detective as well as critic—Joanne Seiden, my secretary. Like any good browser, she was not content to look for the specific book I'd ordered. She would always look on adjacent shelves, research the author's other works, track down bibliographies, and thumb through card catalogues. Thus on every excursion she brought back more selections and more leads. She was also the first audience for any of my selections—the first one to say how a piece 'felt' or whether my excerpting 'worked.'

And so to all of you who gave me leads, to Phil who encouraged and edited, to Joanne who searched and critiqued

Thank you,

Irving Kenneth Zola

Brandeis University
and
Boston Self Help Center

Spastics
by Vassar Miller

They are not beautiful, young, and
strong when it strikes,
but wizened in wombs like everyone else,
like monkeys,
like fish,
like worms,
creepy-crawlies from yesterday's rocks
tomorrow will step on.

Hence presidents, and most parents, don't have to
worry
No one in congress will die of it. No one else.
Don't worry.
They just
hang on
drooling, stupid from watching too much TV,
born-that-way senile,

rarely marry, expected to make it with Jesus,
never really make it at all,
don't know how,
some can't
feed themselves,
fool with, *well*—Even some sappy saint said they
look young because pure.

I

From *Cotton in my Ears*
Frances Warfield

I grew up in Missouri, in the suburbs of St. Louis, in a household of two aunts and three older sisters. We were the four poor rich Warfield girls—poor because we had no parents, rich because our father had been a rich man and we lived in a big white house with tall white Corinthian columns. We were the wards of the St. Louis Trust Company and Aunt Harriet and Aunt May were our guardians.

I was soft and soft-spoken, the beloved baby, the last one, the little one, the poor little one who couldn't remember her mother. I thought my mother had died long before I was born—she must have, because everyone was so sorry for me. Actually, she died when I was one year old. My father died when I was four. I had no memory of him, either, but I associated him in my mind with Old Mr. Bascomb, who had fought in the Civil War and lived not far from our house at the Old Soldiers' Home. Mr. Bascomb was a deaf man. He had been blind and deaf ever since the Battle of Antietam. His face had a blank, vacant expression, and I had heard Aunt Harriet say Old Mr. Bascomb was so stone-deaf he might as well be dead. The words "dead" and "deaf" sounded very much alike to me. I was always getting the two of them mixed up.

Sitting on people's laps or on my special round needle-point footstool beside somebody's chair, I listened intently to grown-up conversation. Often I knew what the grownups were going to want and fetched it without waiting to be told. I came before I was called, sometimes answered questions before they were asked. This was to prove I was as smart and heard as perfectly as my sister Ann did, perhaps even more perfectly.

They called me a dear, sweet, lovely child, and I was. They also called me a funny little monkey, because I pronounced long words they way they sounded.

"Goodness gracious, I'm a radish!" I would exclaim.

It brought the house down. Where on earth did the funny little monkey get her words? Had I heard someone say, "I'm erratic," perhaps?

My oldest sister begged the aunts to let me come downstairs in my bathrobe and slippers and tell her newest beau I was a radish. My second sister wrote an English composition about my being a radish and brought it home from school marked "Excellent." My sister Ann said radishes were silly and made up funny mistakes of her own—reciting "Mary, Mary, white canary" whenever anybody was listening.

As long as the family laughed at me, that meant they liked me. It meant they hadn't discovered my secret and I was safe. I resolved to be very funny as well as very good until I was seven and my adenoids were taken out. After that I wouldn't be so good all the time. My sisters were constantly getting in and out of hot water; their lives seemed fuller than mine. When I was seven and could hear the grass grow like everybody else I wouldn't need to be such an all-fired little angel.

I had a private hideaway behind some lilac bushes in a corner of our yard, where I pursued a secret ritual.

Eyes closed, fingers in my ears, I would repeat the word "wrinkelstiltskin" seven times. It was a magic formula that was to help me hear the grass grow.

One day my sister Ann surprised me testing my magic: I was crouched in my hideaway with one ear pressed to the ground.

"What you doing—playing Indian? I'll play, too."

Ann was several years older than I was and had long thick black braids, whereas my hair was short and brown and too fine to amount to much. Ann knew a lot. As Indians, she instructed, we must keep an ear to the ground and spring up with wild war whoops when we heard the approaching hoofbeats of enemy palefaces. Later on I must be an enemy paleface, she said, and she, the Indian, would scalp what little hair I had right off my head.

When we had whooped and scalped a good while I brought the conversation around to the all-important subject.

"Can you hear the grass grow?" I asked, offhand.

"Oh, sure." Ann polished off a war whoop in mid-air and spun on her heels, her shiny braids swinging straight out from her head. "Can't you?"

Her live black eyes devilish, she dropped to the grass and held her head tipped sidewise, listening.

"Why, goodness gracious, anybody can hear the grass grow," she jeered. "Mean to say *you* can't?"

"I can hear it," I told her firmly. "I can hear it perfectly if I listen."

I mustn't let on I couldn't hear perfectly. People didn't like it. It made them scornful like Ann or exasperated like Aunt May and Aunt Harriet when they called and I didn't answer right away.

"She doesn't always answer when we call," Aunt Harriet had told our family doctor a few days before.

"Do you think the child may not hear well? Do you think that attack of scarlet fever last year can have affected her hearing?"

"Doesn't answer, eh?" Dr. Benedict had given my ear an affectionate pinch and pulled his huge turnip watch from his pocket. "Maybe that depends on what they're calling her for. Suppose it's a whopping dish of chocolate ice cream—any trouble hearing about that?"

He held his watch a foot or so from my ear, and of course I said I heard the watch tick. I wasn't sure I heard it, but I would have sworn I heard hell's bells to please Dr. Benedict. He was such a nice man—big, rumble-throated, smelling like soap and harness leather; I dearly loved him and planned to marry him. A year before, when I'd been five and sick with scarlet fever, I'd hoped he was my father. But I knew better, now that I was six. My father was a dead man. I didn't know what dead was, except some people were dead and gone. They were not in our family any more. Possibly they had not been wanted in our family, for some good reason. Possibly they had something permanently the matter with them. Possibly they had been sent away for that reason.

"She hears all right if she listens." Dr. Benedict nodded. "How old is she—six? Well, let's see—suppose she's very, very good until she's seven. If she is, perhaps we'll take her adenoids out. How would you like that, Miss Cotton Ears? Once we get rid of those adenoids you'll be hearing the grass grow."

I must listen. The doctor said I could hear all right if I listened. But even if I didn't hear I must pretend I did. It wasn't nice not to hear. It wasn't polite. People didn't like it.

The doctor's watch was easy. It was like the

approaching hoofbeats of enemy palefaces when Ann and I played Indian; I could pretend I heard that. Voices were harder because I was supposed to answer and do what they told me to do. Aunt Harriet was easier to hear than Aunt May. Aunt Harriet was tall and straight and formidable and white-haired and spoke sharply. Aunt May was round and rosy-faced and pleasant and her voice was too mild for comfort.

I must listen hard. Sometimes, when I didn't hear at first, it would flash over me, a second later, what had been said. I must never look blank. No matter how much I wanted to, I must never say "What?" "What?" was perilous. "What?" would give away my secret and I'd be exposed to deadly danger.

I could guess what would happen if Aunt Harriet and Aunt May found out the truth. If they made up their minds I really couldn't hear perfectly, they wouldn't want me. That was the deadly danger. They would have me called for by the Charity Guild wagon that stopped at the back door on Tuesdays if you sent word you had something to be called for.

"This child is imperfect," Aunt Harriet would explain to Aunt May. Perhaps she would simply write "For the Charity Guild" on a slip of paper, pin the paper to the collar of my dress, and set me out on the back porch steps.

Where would I be taken? To some poor family. Some poor tenement family that had to be satisfied with what children it could get. Or to an orphans' home. After all, I was a poor little orphan—everyone said so. Orphans were safe in our family if they were older, like my two older sisters, or knew a lot and had beautiful thick black braids, like my sister Ann, or were dear, sweet and lovely, like me. But a poor little orphan who couldn't hear the grass grow was on thin ice until she was seven and her adenoids were taken out.

It was a lucky thing my not hearing the grass grow was only temporary. If it were permanent, I'd have been sent away long ago. Naturally. A rich family like ours didn't keep people around who had anything permanently the matter with them. Why should they? I must listen until I was seven. I must repeat the magic word "wrinkelstiltskin" seven times every day, seven days every week. I must never let on to anyone—especially to my sister Ann, who might very well betray me—that I couldn't hear absolutely everything.

There was one thing I could hear that Ann couldn't. It was the sound of the ocean—a faint roaring in my ears that I got from a pale pink sea shell Mrs. George Furness brought Ann and me from the East, marked "Souvenir of Rye Beach, New Hampshire." "Hold it to your ear," Ann had directed. "You can hear the sound of the ocean."

Because the shell had come out of the ocean, Ann said, it had the sound of the ocean inside it forever after. I put it to my ear and I could hear the sound—a faint roaring that grew louder as I listened.

"I hear it," I said excitedly. "I hear it forever after!"

This was true. When I took the shell away I could still hear the roaring sound, in both my ears.

"Do you hear it forever after—do you?" I asked Ann. "Does everybody hear the ocean forever after who listens to the shell?"

Ann put the shell to her own ear. "They hear it forever after if they want to," she said. She took the shell away from her ear, and I could tell from her face she didn't hear the roaring any more. "And if they don't," she decided, spinning around on her heels, "they don't care if they do or not."

Wrinkel came along at this time. I wanted a close friend. Also, in my world of aunts and sisters, a boy was interesting.

Wrinkel was invisible and inaudible, which left him free to do and say whatever he wanted. The first time he entered a room he found the exact center of the ceiling and drove in a large invisible staple. He tossed an invisible rope ladder through the staple, festooning it over the tops of pictures, curtain poles, and chandeliers, and climbed over people's heads, listening to their talk and making nonsense of it.

Wrinkel was smarter than anybody—smarter than my sister Ann. For one thing, he was a boy. For another thing, though he could hear as perfectly as Ann could, he didn't care whether he heard perfectly or not. He chose to hear, and to act on what he heard, strictly as he had a mind to.

No one ever jeered at a little boy like Wrinkel. If our cook ever asked him to gather about fifteen apples from under the tree in the yard and he gathered about fifty, Ann wouldn't make fun of him for gathering such a big pile. She'd know Wrinkel distinctly heard the cook ask for fifteen apples but decided, on his own, to gather about fifty. If Aunt Harriet ever sent Wrinkel to her room for the shears and he fetched shoes instead, Aunt Harriet would be respectful. She'd know Wrinkel preferred to fetch shoes, or fetched shoes for a joke; in any case, she'd know he knew all along it was shears he'd been sent for.

Wrinkel kept me safe from danger. When somebody said something to me and I didn't hear it, all I had to do

was say, "Wrinkel, oh, Wrinkel, let down your hair!"
I'd say it as fast as I could, running the words together.
It didn't mean anything—that was the fun of it. When I
said "Wrinkelohwrinkelletdownyourhair!" it made the
grownups laugh and call me a funny little monkey and
the danger of exposure was averted.

When people talked and talked and Wrinkel didn't
make sense of what they said, that wasn't because he
didn't hear it. It was because he liked to make
nonsense by weaving his own name in and out of their
sentences.

"It gives me great pleasure to wrinkeluce Mrs.
Wrinkel O'Wrinkelman." thus, the plump, breathy-
voiced chairman of my aunts' Thursday Club, standing
behind our big, heavily carved library table while I sat
on my needle-point footstool beside Aunt Harriet's
chair and Wrinkel climbed the chandelier. "Mrs.
O'Wrinkelman has recently wrinkelurned from
wrinkteen wrinks of wrissionary work in China."

In church on Sundays the invisible Wrinkel swung
unconcernedly on his rope ladder and climbed in and
out among the highest rafters, enduring the offertory
anthem ("As the wrink panteth after the
wrinkelbrook"), ignoring the prayers ("We have
wrinked those wranks which we ought not to have
wrunk"), giving scant heed to the long-winded sermon
on the wrinketh chapter of the wrinkeleth verse of the
Gospel according to St. Wrinkthew. Straddling the
arch above the church doorway as the congregation
filed out, he would mimic soundlessly and mock-
solemnly, "Good wrinking, Miss Wrinkeldine—the
wrinkatism's better, I hope?" "No better, Mr. Wrinker,
but you're kind to wrinquire."

Wrinkel and I had a lot in common. Invisibility, for
one thing. Mouse-quiet in a room full of chattering

people, I often felt invisible. Then, too, I knew what it was to feel inaudible. Aunt Harriet sometimes told me rather sharply to speak up. I couldn't answer her back, because it wasn't polite, but Wrinkel could. If anyone ever told a little boy like Wrinkel to speak up he'd have jeered, "What's the matter—cotton in your ears?"

Those were the Seven Deadly Words: "What's the matter—cotton in your ears?" If anybody ever said those words to me, it would kill me. It would mean the whole world knew the secret thing about me, that I didn't always hear perfectly. That would be the end.

The deadly words were safe with Wrinkel. He'd never use them against a close friend like me. He'd use them only to kill the people he and I agreed on.

He killed people off for me all the time. He killed off all the ones I didn't like—the ones who cleared their throats pointedly or raised their voices at me, as if they thought I might not hear them. He killed off deadpans, when they mumbled some question at me. I'd mumble an answer and when they said the perilous "What?"—that was the signal for Wrinkel to kill them invisibly and inaudibly with the Seven Deadly Words. It was dangerous to kill people, but a little boy like Wrinkel could do it if he wanted to. He was invisible and inaudible; no one could kill him back.

I killed only one person myself, and that was Old Mr. Bascomb. I up and killed him on Memorial Day, at the gateway of the Old Soldiers' Home. He had ridden in the Memorial Day parade and looked proud and distinguisehd in his Civil War uniform and his hat with gold cord on it.

It took courage to walk past him all alone. My ears set up their sea-shell roaring, which always got louder when I was scared. I was terribly afraid of deaf people—they didn't like me; I couldn't talk loud enough; I was too shy. Moreover, I thought they might be on to my secret. I thought that, being deaf themselves, perhaps they could tell by looking at me I didn't always hear.

However, as I passed Old Mr. Bascomb that Memorial Day afternoon, I suddenly realized I didn't have to be afraid of him. He was blind. He couldn't see me any more than he could hear me. He stood at the gateway of the Old Soldiers' Home, still wearing his uniform, smiling a little in the sun, and I stood looking up at him, wondering if he knew I was there. He didn't seem to. I was as invisible and inaudible as Wrinkel. It occurred to me to kill Old Mr. Bascomb off, because, as Aunt Harriet had said, he was so stone-deaf he might as well be dead—so I looked straight into his face and said, quite loud, "What's—the matter—cotton in your ears?"

It was exciting, and perfectly safe. Old Mr. Bascomb's blank, vacant stare didn't change. He was a dead man. I had killed him with the Seven Deadly Words. I ran home feeling good. I felt exactly the way a little boy like Wrinkel would feel—strong and brave and full of secret glee.

I was so afraid of deaf people that I dreaded even walking past the old Nye place. It was a square, dark house—one of the biggest in town—at the end of a long avenue of locust trees. There were three deaf people there—Old Mrs. Nye and her daughters, Miss Eva Nye and Mrs. George Furness.

Everyone said Mrs. Furness was wonderful and bore her affliction bravely. And everyone said Mr. George Furness had the patience of a saint, going through life with his mouth glued to the end of his wife's ear trumpet. She had several trumpets—a tortoise-shell one and a silver one shaped like a coffee pot. (She put the spout in her ear.) Her favorite was a black one shaped like a hunting horn; it was dented and scratched and had traveled East to Rye Beach, New Hampshire, with her every summer for twenty years.

Mrs. Nye was so old and so deaf that an ear trumpet couldn't do her any good. Miss Eva wasn't as hard of hearing as her mother and sister, but everyone wished she'd give in and face reality and get an ear trumpet like Mrs. Furness instead of pretending like a silly ostrich that she could hear perfectly if people would only speak distinctly. Aunt May often laughed about the time she sold Miss Eva three tickets to a Charity Guild concert and had to pay for them out of her own pocket. Miss Eva understood her to say "free tickets" not "three tickets," and it was too hard to explain, especially since everyone knew that, for all their money, the Nyes were close and Miss Eva was sometimes suspected of using her deafness as a convenience.

When we were sent on errands to the Nye house I would try to make my sister Ann go up to the door while I waited at the gate. I don't know which of the three women I was most afraid of—Miss Eva, who snapped my head off for mumbling, or Mrs. Furness, who pointed her big black ear trumpet at me, or Mrs. Nye, who stared blankly no matter how hard I tried to shout. I guess I was most afraid of Mrs. Furness, though I was fascinated, at the same time, by her ear trumpet and the electric earphone in her pew in church.

I gathered that when Mrs. Furness put her hunting horn in ther ear it made everything sound very loud; possibly it brought sounds from far away that other people couldn't hear. I wanted very much to put the horn in my own ear and find out what happened, though I wouldn't have wanted anyone to catch me doing it. I was always hoping Mrs. Furness would forget and leave it at our house so I could sneak a listen when nobody was looking, but she never did. However, I did once sneak a listen from the earphone she had in church.

I didn't know the earphone was attached to an electric amplifier and transmitter on the pulpit and that the rector switched it off and on. I assumed that, since Mrs. Furness kept this earphone in church, it was connected with God. One day, when I was sent to look for a letter Aunt May thought she might have left in her hymnbook, I had a chance to try it out.

It felt sacreligious to walk into the dim, empty church on a weekday and I held my breath with fear as I tiptoed to the Nye pew, lifted the earphone off its hook, and put it cautiously to my ear. I didn't hear anything except the sea shell roaring in my own ears, which always got louder when I was scared. The earphone wasn't working. God's earphones, apparently, worked on Sundays only.

As Dr. Benedict had ordered, I was very, very good until I was seven and my adenoids were taken out. Also, I pursued my secret magic ritual. Crouched in my hideaway behind the lilac bushes in the yard, I closed my eyes and put my fingers in my ears and repeated "wrinkelstiltskin" seven times every day. I even devised finer and fancier magic, such as avoiding cracks in the pavement and touching every other railing of every fence I ever passed.

"Can you hear now?" my sister Ann wanted to know, as soon as my adenoids had been taken out. "Can you hear perfectly?"

I nodded. My throat was too sore for me to say anything. I was sitting up in bed with an ice collar around my neck eating cracked ice out of a bowl. Nothing had happened. Instead of feeling keen as an Indian brave's, my hearing felt as usual, cottony around the edges. But naturally I wasn't letting on to Ann.

"I bet you can't," she said. "I bet you're deaf. I bet you're deaf."

She swung her braids and spun around on her heels. I wished Wrinkel were there. If Wrinkel had been there, he would have killed Ann off for me.

And The Children Shall Lead Us
Irving Kenneth Zola

It was freezing cold. I sat huddled behind the wheel of my car waiting, as I do every Wednesday, for Amanda to get out of school. The radio was blaring, the heater was rumbling, and I was absorbed in a paperback novel, so I didn't hear the first knock. With the second, I saw Amanda pointing to the window. Anything that let the cold in seemed outrageous, so I only opened it a crack.

"Daddy, you're such a silly," she said with a certain exasperation. "I meant the door, not the window!"

To me that seemed silly and I told her so. "You know you can't climb over me that easily. Why don't you go in the back door...like always?"

With a patience that a nine year old develops to deal with the older generation, she gave me a benign smile. "I don't want to come in. I want you to come out." And then, acknowledging with her hand another snow-suited young girl, she explained, "I want you to show Kristin your leg."

"My what?" I stammered in surprise.

"Your leg, the one with the brace," she said off-handedly.

"My leg," I answered softly to no one in particular.

"Yes," she went on, "Kristin often asks me about you and about it. So when she brought it up today, I thought now was a good time."

Her matter-of-factness was almost hypnotic. And so turning in my seat, I first placed my left foot outside and then with my hands lifted my right to join it. And there I sat . . . a grey-bearded forty-four year old clad in an olive-drab parka jacket and his favorite blue jeans.

"Well there it is," said Amanda, pointing triumphantly at my leg. We all looked at it. Amanda, Kristin and another friend who stopped on his way home. The only "it" that was immediately visible was the bottom of my brace, two pieces of shining aluminum attached to the heel of my shoe. Kristin nodded her head and when she falteringly asked, "How, umm, umm. . .?" I knew the question. "You mean, how high does it go?" She nodded again.

"It goes all the way up here," and I traced the brace from my ankle to my hip. Very young children want to touch it and say so, but this older audience said little and so I didn't offer.

"Why do you wear it?" asked the boy.

Amanda smiled, "I've told them about the polio, but," and she pursed her lips and shook her head as if she thought I'd like to tell it again, "you say."

And so I did, telling briefly about polio—a disease already to them a piece of history—something they knew about only indirectly by "the sips they once had to take in school" to avoid having it. But they were more interested in how the brace worked. And so I began to explain, "Because of the weakness in my leg. . .without the brace, my knee would keep bending and I'd fall. But this way," and I patted it, "the brace keeps my leg stiff and unbending."

"You know Daddy. Your leg doesn't look weak. I mean," and she waved toward both of them, "they look the same to me."

"You're right," I laughed, a little nervously. This was a question I'd never been asked. "They are almost the same. But if you look close—some day when I'm not wearing the brace, I'll show you—the right leg is a little thinner than the left. And. . . if you look at me carefully in shorts you'll see that I'm pretty big all around here," and I let my hands fall across my rather thick chest, "but that I'm much thinner below the waist."

This clicked off a memory in Amanda and she turned to her two friends, "The other day my daddy and I were in a restaurant and we saw a waitress without a real leg." The two children gazed at her disbelievingly. "She had something else. I don't know what you call it. I think it was made of wood or plastic and looked sort of like a real leg but not exactly. I know you're not supposed to stare, but my Daddy said it was better to be curious than be uncomfortable and look away. . . ." And then with a conclusive sigh, "It was amazing. She did real well," and nodded her head approvingly.

Her friends agreed and looked toward me.

"Do you have any more questions?" Amanda said in her most teacherly fashion. "No," they nodded and smiling at both of us whispered, "thank you," and trotted away in the snow.

Amanda, with an air of satisfaction, settled in the back seat. I turned around and asked what that was all about. "Well, Kristin often asks me questions about you and about your leg. And when she asked again today, I thought you could do it better."

"Better?"

"Yes, there's only so much I could say. Some things you have to see."

"Oh," I answered rather speechlessly.

"And besides, I knew you'd oblige."

"Oblige?" I laughed at her choice of words.

"Yes," and she gave me a coy look. tilting her head downward, "I thought you'd be comfortable doing it. You were, weren't you?"

As I shifted the car to start, I nodded "Yes." But to myself I added... "and every day I get a little more comfortable."

From *My Left Foot*
Christy Brown

I was born in the Rotunda Hospital, on June 5th, 1932. There were nine children before me and twelve after me, so I myself belong to the middle group. Out of this total of twenty-two, seventeen lived, but four died in infancy, leaving thirteen still to hold the family fort.

Mine was a difficult birth, I am told. Both mother and son almost died. A whole army of relations queued up outside the hospital until the small hours of the morning, waiting for news and praying furiously that it would be good.

After my birth mother was sent to recuperate for some weeks and I was kept in the hospital while she was away. I remained there for some time, without name, for I wasn't baptized until my mother was well enough to bring me to church.

It was mother who first saw that there was something wrong with me. I was about four months old at the time. She noticed that my head had a habit of falling backward whenever she tried to feed me. She attempted to correct this by placing her hand on the back of my neck to keep it steady. But when she took it away, back it would drop again. That was the first warning sign. Then she became aware of other defects as I got older. She saw that my hands were clenched nearly all of the time and were inclined to twine behind my back, my mouth couldn't grasp the teat of the bottle because even at that early age my jaws would either lock together tightly, so that it was impossible for her to open them, or they would suddenly become limp and fall loose, dragging my whole mouth to one side. At six months I could not sit up without having a mountain of pillows around me. At twelve months it was the same.

Very worried about this, mother told my father her fears, and they decided to seek medical advice without any further delay. I was a little over a year old when they began to take me to hospitals and clinics, convinced that there was something definitely wrong with me, something which they could not understand or name, but which was very real and disturbing.

Almost every doctor who saw and examined me, labeled me a very interesting but also a hopeless case. Many told mother very gently that I was mentally defective and would remain so. That was a hard blow to a young mother who had already reared five healthy children. The doctors were so very sure of themselves that mother's faith in me seemed almost an impertinence. They assured her that nothing could be done for me.

She refused to accept this truth, the inevitable truth—as it then seemed—that I was beyond cure, beyond saving, even beyond hope. She could not and would not believe that I was an imbecile, as the doctors told her. She had nothing in the world to go by, not a scrap of evidence to support her conviction that, though my body was crippled, my mind was not. In spite of all the doctors and specialists told her, she would not agree. I don't believe she knew why—she just knew, without feeling the smallest shade of doubt.

Finding that the doctors could not help in any way beyond telling her not to place her trust in me, or, in other words, to forget I was a human creature, rather to regard me as just something to be fed and washed and then put away again, mother decided there and then to take matters into her own hands. I was *her* child, and therefore part of the family. No matter how dull and incapable I might grow up to be, she was determined to treat me on the same plane as the others, and not as the "queer one" in the back room who was never spoken of when there were visitors present.

That was a momentous decision as far as my future life was concerned. It meant that I would always have my mother on my side to help me fight all the battles that were to come, and to inspire me with new strength when I was almost beaten. But it wasn't easy for her because now the relatives and friends had decided otherwise. They contended that I should be taken kindly, sympathetically, but not seriously. That would be a mistake. "For your own sake," they told her, "don't look to this boy as you would to the others; it would only break your heart in the end." Luckily for me, mother and father held out against the lot of them. But mother wasn't content just to say that I was not an idiot: she set out to prove it, not because of any rigid sense of duty, but out of love. That is why she was so successful.

At this time she had the five other children to look after besides the "difficult one," though as yet it was not by any means a full house. They were my brothers, Jim, Tony, and Paddy, and my two sisters, Lily and Mona, all of them very young, just a year or so between each of them, so that they were almost exactly like steps of stairs.

Four years rolled by and I was now five, and still as helpless as a newly born baby. While my father was out at bricklaying, earning our bread and butter for us, mother was slowly, patiently pulling down the wall, brick by brick, that seemed to thrust itself between me and the other children, slowly, patiently penetrating beyond the thick curtain that hung over my mind, separating it from theirs. It was hard, heartbreaking work, for often all she got from me in return was a vague smile and perhaps a faint gurgle. I could not speak or even mumble, nor could I sit up without support on my own, let alone take steps. But I wasn't inert or motionless. I seemed, indeed, to be convulsed with movement, wild, stiff, snakelike movement that never left me, except in sleep. My fingers twisted and twitched continually, my arms twined backwards and would often shoot out suddenly this way and that, and my head lolled and sagged sideways. I was a queer, crooked little fellow.

Mother tells me how one day she had been sitting with me for hours in an upstairs room, showing me pictures out of a great big storybook that I had got from Santa Claus last Christmas and telling me the names of the different animals and flowers that were in them, trying without success to get me to repeat them. This had gone on for hours while she talked and laughed with me. Then at the end of it she leaned over me and said gently into my ear:

"Did you like it, Chris? Did you like the bears and the monkeys and all the lovely flowers? Nod your head for yes, like a good boy."

But I could make no sign that I had understood her. Her face was bent over mine hopefully. Suddenly, involuntarily, my queer hand reached up and grasped one of the dark curls that fell in a thick cluster about her neck. Gently she loosened the clenched fingers, though some dark strands were still clutched between them.

Then she turned away from my curious stare and left the room, crying. The door closed behind her. It all seemed hopeless. It looked as though there was some justification for my relatives' contention that I was an idiot and beyond help.

They now spoke of an institution.

"Never!" said my mother almost fiercely, when this was suggested to her. "I know my boy is not an idiot. It is his body that is shattered, not his mind. I'm sure of that."

Sure? Yet inwardly, she prayed God would give her some proof of her faith. She knew it was one thing to believe but quite another thing to prove.

I was now five, and still I showed no real sign of intelligence. I showed no apparent interest in things except with my toes—more especially those of my left foot. Although my natural habits were clean, I could not aid myself, but in this respect my father took care of me. I used to lie on my back all the time in the kitchen or, on bright warm days, out in the garden, a little bundle of crooked muscles and twisted nerves, surrounded by a family that loved me and hoped for me and that made me part of their own warmth and humanity. I was lonely, imprisoned in a world of my own, unable to communicate with others, cut off, separated from them as though a glass wall stood between my existence and theirs, thrusting me beyond the sphere of their lives and activities. I longed to run about and play with the rest, but I was unable to break loose from my bondage.

Then, suddenly, it happened! In a moment everything was changed, my future life molded into a definite shape, my mother's faith in me rewarded and her secret fear changed into open triumph.

It happened so quickly, so simply after all the years of waiting and uncertainty, that I can see and feel the whole scene as if it had happened last week. It was the afternoon of a cold, gray December day. The streets outside glistened with snow, the white sparkling flakes stuck and melted on the windowpanes and hung on the boughs of the trees like molten silver. The wind howled dismally, whipping up little whirling columns of snow that rose and fell at every fresh gust. And over all, the dull, murky sky stretched like a dark canopy, a vast infinity of grayness.

Inside, all the family were gathered round the big kitchen fire that lit up the little room with a warm glow and made giant shadows dance on the walls and ceiling.

In a corner Mona and Paddy were sitting, huddled together, a few torn school primers before them. They were writing down little sums on to an old chipped slate, using a bright piece of yellow chalk. I was close to them, propped up by a few pillows against the wall, watching.

It was the chalk that attracted me so much. It was a long, slender stick of vivid yellow. I had never seen anything like it before, and it showed up so well against the black surface of the slate that I was fascinated by it as much as if it had been a stick of gold.

Suddenly, I wanted desperately to do what my sister was doing. Then—without thinking or knowing exactly what I was doing, I reached out and took the stick of chalk out of my sister's hand—with my left foot.

I do not know why I used my left foot to do this. It is a puzzle to many people as well as to myself, for, although I had displayed a curious interest in my toes at an early age, I had never attempted before this to use either of my feet in any way. They could have been as useless to me as were my hands. That day, however, my left foot, apparently by its own volition, reached out and very impolitely took the chalk out of my sister's hand.

I held it tightly between my toes, and, acting on an impulse, made a wild sort of scribble with it on the slate. Next moment I stopped, a bit dazed, surprised, looking down at the stick of yellow chalk stuck between my toes, not knowing what to do with it next, hardly knowing how it got there. Then I looked up and became aware that everyone had stopped talking and was staring at me silently. Nobody stirred. Mona, her black curls framing her chubby little face, stared at me with great big eyes and open mouth. Across the open hearth, his face lit by flames, sat my father, leaning forward, hands outspread on his knees, his shoulders tense. I felt the sweat break out on my forehead.

My mother came in from the pantry with a steaming pot in her hand. She stopped midway between the table and the fire, feeling the tension flowing through the room. She followed their stare and saw me in the corner. Her eyes looked from my face down to my foot, with the chalk gripped between my toes. She put down the pot.

Then she crossed over to me and knelt down beside me, as she had done so many times before.

"I'll show you what to do with it, Chris," she said, very slowly and in a queer, choked way, her face flushed as if with some inner excitement.

Taking another piece of chalk from Mona, she hesitated, then very deliberately drew, on the floor in front of me *the single letter "A."*

"Copy that," she said, looking steadily at me. "Copy it, Christy."

I couldn't.

I looked about me, looked around at the faces that were turned towards me, tense, excited faces that were at that moment frozen, immobile, eager, waiting for a miracle in their midst.

The stillness was profound. The room was full of flame and shadow that danced before my eyes and lulled my taut nerves into a sort of waking sleep. I could hear the sound of the water tap dripping in the pantry, the loud ticking of the clock on the mantelshelf, and the soft hiss and crackle of the logs on the open hearth.

I tried again. I put out my foot and made a wild jerking stab with the chalk which produced a very crooked line and nothing more. Mother held the slate steady for me.

"Try again, Chris," she whispered in my ear. "Again."

I did. I stiffened my body and put my left foot out again, for the third time. I drew one side of the letter. I drew half the other side. Then the stick of chalk broke and I was left with a stump. I wanted to fling it away and give up. Then I felt my mother's hand on my shoulder. I tried once more. Out went my foot. I shook, I sweated and strained every muscle. My hands were so tightly clenched that my fingernails bit into the flesh. I set my teeth so hard that I nearly pierced my lower lip. Everything in the room swam till the faces around me were mere patches of white. But—I drew it—*the letter "A."* There it was on the floor before me. Shaky, with awkward, wobbly sides and a very uneven center line. But it *was* the letter "A." I looked up. I saw my mother's face for a moment, tears on her cheeks. Then my father stooped and hoisted me on to his shoulder.

I had done it! It had started—the thing that was to give my mind its chance of expressing itself. True, I couldn't speak with my lips. But now I would speak through something more lasting than spoken words—written words.

That one letter, scrawled on the floor with a broken bit of yellow chalk gripped between my toes, was my road to a new world, my key to mental freedom. It was to provide a source of relaxation to the tense, taut thing that was I, which panted for expression behind a twisted mouth.

From *The Long Walk Home*
Leonard Kriegel

Cape Cod, the summer. Smell of salt and sand, raucous gull whose grace I envied, feel of sun burning into my brow as I dawdled days away lying on an old wharf bench, homage to Eugene O'Neill and Provincetown splinters, nights spent staring out at the sea, bright moon above me a sponge for the world. And then Helen, one night with Helen that was to creep like paralysis through my selfhood.

There was a performance that night and Helen accompanied some friends onto the wharf. I was sitting there; it was where I had taken to going since my first day in Provincetown. Helen sat down beside me on the wooden bench and stared out to sea. The evening was heavy with the smell of the sea, and the prospect of sharing it with anyone was not to my liking. I would have preferred the bench for myself. But it wasn't mine to claim.

She was about ten years older than I was, a tall, well-built woman. She didn't speak until the crowd on the wharf had gone inside the theater. Then she asked me for a light, even though I could see the matches folded into the cellophane of her cigarette pack, a rare practice in a woman. "I didn't have a ticket," she explained. "Anyway, this night...I'd rather be out here." She paused and dragged on the cigarette. "It's beautiful. Isn't it beautiful?"

"Yes," I agreed.

She leaned down and touched one of the crutches, which were lying lengthwise below the bench. "How long have you had them?"

"Years," I said. "More than eight years now."

She continued to smoke, her left hand inching across the bench until it flattened itself out on my hip. What she wanted was to feel the leather. Okay, if she wanted to feel the leather, then I would give her the leather to feel. And more, too. "I have a son," she announced, as my hand slid over hers. I fondled her hand. There was a slight roughness to her hand that made the heat rise in me. But then she was staring out into the bay, as if she had deliberately chosen this moment to detach herself from my eagerness. "His name is Paulie. I think he looks like you."

His name is Paulie. Fine. I think he looks like you. Better. Lady, I want to give you a. . . . "That's nice," I answered, not knowing what else to say.

"He's six and a half." She paused. "He's spastic. My husband's mother, she says it's a curse." She was staring at the water, at the reflection of the moon and the silhouettes of the Portuguese fishing boats lying at anchor in the middle of the bay.

"That's stupid," I said, dropping her hand. My tongue running across my lips, I searched for something else to say. "Your husband's mother is crazy."

"Do people stare at you?" A few strands of black hair fell across that broad, conscious forehead, whetstone for my desire.

"Sure. So what? Look, it doesn't matter, does it? I'm sorry about your son." There was a narrow precision about the way she sat on the bench that disturbed me. "What's your name?"

"Helen," she answered, still staring out at the bay. "What's yours?"

"Lennie."

Neither of us spoke for the next few minutes. "Why does every man at the hotel want to make me?" she asked abruptly. I wanted to reach out and slap so childish a view of the universe, but I just grabbed the edge of the bench and held on tight. "All men think that if a woman is alone, she's trash. A man wants nothing but to have his way. I'm married."

"Maybe you want a drink," I offered. "There's a bar down the street. It's quiet."

"I hate my husband. But I'd like my son to grow up and not feel it," she announced, staring now at the wooden railing in front of us. "Like you. Being crippled isn't a handicap for you, is it?"

"I'm sorry about your son," I repeated. "I really am." My very embarrassment had somehow made me even more desirous of making the connection with her. "Come with me for a drink. We'll talk about whatever you want—your son even."

"The water," she said, "it's beautiful. Look at the way the boats rock." She dropped her hand on my knee again. "Steel?" she asked, fingering the locks.

Lover. Great man of a lover. And all that happened was that she played with my braces. "Do you have a car?" I asked.

She removed her hand from my knee. "It's really not so terrible, is it? Being a spastic."

"He'll be fine," I said. It was the cheapest thing to say.

"But it's not so good, either. The kids make fun of him."

"For Christ's sake, Helen."

"I'm sorry. We'll go. My car's down the road."

We left the wharf, walking slowly. The smell of salt air stabbed the smell of her perfume. Her son, a spastic. A spastic. Anyway, how could I measure her pain? She was the way she was and that was all. She made me feel ashamed of myself and hot for her at the same time, as if the shame in some weird way made the desire even greater. A new angle on being crippled. And what would Hemingway say to this? I love you because you smell the disease in me. Oh, Papa Ernie, everybody bleeds.

We drove up to Race Point, at the farthest end of the Cape. I could see the fires burning on the beach, like occasional fireflies. The thought of all those bodies writhing in the menace of satisfaction was oil for my flame. At Race Point, where we could go no farther, where ocean and bay joined together in an angry reminder, for me, of how deeply I shared my cripple with others, Helen stopped the car. She lit a cigarette, her lips trembling. For the moment, the night had engulfed my desire, and the sound of waves crashing against the shore was dampening to my heat. But that was just for the moment. There were also the fires and the bodies on the beach.

"I am not going to listen," Helen suddenly insisted.

"To who?"

"To her. It's not a curse. It's nothing. An accident of birth, that's all. For God's sake, he's nothing but a child. What does she want from me?"

I suppose I wasn't oblivious to my advantage. And yet I would be lying were I to claim that this is what I thought of. It was as if, for the first time since that April day, I was able to reach out and touch the terror in another human being, to soothe a wound that was, in some mysterious way, my wound, too. I pulled her to me and held her. Even later, after we had broken

through into the brittle assurance of night, I was left filled with her pain.

Hours later, we drove back to Provincetown. "I
hope he's like you," Helen said, over and over again,
as the car plowed through the New England darkness.
"Like you. Like you." I felt sick, and when Helen dropped me in front of the boarding house at which I was
staying, the first thing I did, upon entering the house,
was to make my way to the john and stand over the
toilet until I threw up. I sweated it out for a long time,
as if I had a fever, and then, feeling better, washed up
and began to make my way back to my room. I had to
go through the sitting room, the walls of which were
covered with pictures of Jesus—Jesus smiling benign-
ly, Jesus sad, Jesus blessing a woman on her knees in
front of him, Jesus gazing heavenwards, halo around
his head.

I opened the door to my room and went inside. I lay
down on the bed, still clothed, the straps on my
kneecaps beginning to cut into the flesh. I looked at my
watch. It was past two. I switched the night lamp on. It
was a cheap lamp, brass stem topped by a paper
shade, a bulb that did not give very much light. There
was a damp smell to the room. "God," I whispered,
"what a world you made for people."

There was another Jesus on the wall. This one was
wearing a white robe, staring up at the dirty yellow ceiling. He stood, in all his five-and-ten-cent piety, against
a purple background. A metal bowl protruded from the
bottom of the maple frame. Jesus, with the *pishka*,
beggar for all the souls in this world. My grandmother,
she would understand. *Jesus with the Pishka: A Study
for the Grandeur of Man Against Purple.* I removed my
watch from my wrist, then emptied my pockets of

wallet, cigarettes, keys, handkerchief, and loose change. I switched off the light and lay in the darkness, still clothed, my braces still strapped to my legs. From the world outside, I could hear an occasional car engine bearing the world into the Elysian victories of Race Point darkness. "A spastic," I said to the darkness. "Do you hear me, Jesus?" I switched on the lamp and sat up in bed, eyeing my Jesus on the wall. Then I lit a cigarette and puffed the smoke in his direction. I counted my change—three nickels, two dimes, four pennies. Thirty-nine cents. I began to flip the coins, one after the other, at the tin bowl fastened to my Jesus on the wall. "Here," I whispered. "You're God, no?" So I'll buy his body from you. his body, my money." But the Begging Jesus did nothing but continue to smile. For the moment, I believed, really believed, that he was the son of God, and after I had flipped the last coin I was afraid, deathly afraid. But I undressed anyway, took off my braces, and went to sleep.

From *Ordinary Daylight*
Andrew Potok

On a bright August afternoon...Charlotte deposited me at St. Paul's Rehabilitation Center in Newton, Massachusetts. I had become incapable of dealing with my approaching blindness, and I signed up for a four-month residency with others also going blind. We all wanted to learn, with varying degrees of desperation, how to survive. It was my first contact with blind people and with the extensive blindness empire.

St. Paul's Rehabilitation Center for Newly Blinded Adults had in its name the most revolting connotations. I imagined Spencer Tracy in *Boys' Town*, silent, busy nuns in bare-bulbed corridors, forlorn clinics with nailed-down furniture, fluorescent green offices stacked with case loads. But as difficult as the word *rehabilitation* was to handle, the word *blind* was worse. It was fraught with archetypal nightmares: beggars with tin cups, the useless, helpless, hopeless dregs of humanity. It was a word I still couldn't say, not to my friends or my family, and when Dr. Lubkin first said it to me, *speaking of me*, I wanted to scream.

Our old orange VW was crammed with my reel-to-reel tape recorder, the cassette player, tapes of books and music, the bulky, knobby glasses and lenses that for a brief period of time had helped me paint. As Charlotte and I turned off Centre Street at the sign that said *Catholic Guild for All the Blind*, we were surprised by the elegant estate with splendidly manicured lawns, enormous trees, and flowering shrubs. Within the complex of stately old buildings, the parking lot was already filling with candidates for rehabilitation. Family groups with little girls in taffeta, boys in their Sunday best, dogs, parents, old people, clustered around each vehicle. The focus of all this activity, standing in the center of each family constellation, was a slow-moving, clumsy blind person. Self-consciously, almost furtively, Charlotte and I joined the flow.

The Center's staff stood around the entrance to the St. Paul's building, a richly gabled, arched, stone structure, greeting and directing us. They looked perfectly normal, in print dresses or shirt sleeves, smiling, cheerfully shaking hands. There seemed to be no nuns or priests among them, no missionaries or wardens, no life-renouncing shut-ins or ruddy-cheeked fund raisers. There was, rather, a garden-party atmosphere in which the dejected clients-to-be looked strangely out of place, like Hasidic Jews at a DAR convention. As for me, I felt as though I were the strangest of all, in my Vermont Levi's and boots, a three-week stubble of beard sprouting on my face.

I deposited my bags just inside the entrance. Three or four blind people sat there in isolation. They looked broken. Charlotte and I left quickly, managing to avoid the welcoming committees.

"It's pretty here," I said.

"Yes," she agreed, casting frightened glances, her eyes darting, her arms pulling me away from St. Paul's. We walked with short nervous steps over the fancy estate, and all the while, Charlotte eyed her watch and our car in the parking lot.

"Well, Andy," she finally said, "it's time for me to go. I hope this is good for you. It's certainly strange." She left, waving and throwing kisses from the car. Terrified but curious, I was alone, as alone as I'd ever felt in my life.

Inside, a tall, blond man offered to help me bring my belongings upstairs. "I'm a mobility instructor," he said. I recognized him from a St. Paul's brochure.

"Take my arm," he said, and led me upstairs. Seven of us were to live in two converted closets and part of a narrow hallway. He seemed to find nothing extraordinary about these accommodations. "A bit cramped," was all he said, thinking perhaps that the blind are liberated from aesthetic concerns.

"I'll show you how to get to the bathroom," he said, taking my arm firmly. "As you get out of bed," he said, "turn right and take three steps." We did it. "You're now in the hall," he said. Of course I was. I saw the cracked and peeling linoleum, the big old radiator under a large sooty window, the pipes running along the ceilings. "Be careful here," he warned. "You must turn left immediately because of the open staircase. Take three more steps and right again."

"But look," I said apologetically. "I can see the bathroom," pointing to it.

"Well," he said, "you'd better remember anyway," and frowning, he took my hand to place it on the door of the toilet stalls. "Four steps to the left is the shower," he said and bringing my hand along to the sinks: "four washstands."

I felt out of place. I wondered if they had ever dealt with people who could see as much as I could see. Perhaps they had made a mistake accepting me. Again, I was the refugee boy, sent away too early, too scared, too confused. As for blindness, I qualified on paper. And, anyway, I would soon be as blind as they expected.

My sight had been going downhill fast. Print looked as if it had been soaked in a bathtub. On my bad days, it looked eaten by acid. Sometimes, I could see headlines, but even they swam in and out of blind spots. Everything else appeared as in a dazzling snowstorm—gauzy and colorless. Already the blind areas, the scotomas, were widening considerably, like puddles in a heavy rain. I was frightened by the blanks, the no sights, which registered only by the notable absence of things I knew were there. Still, there was so much I could see and do compared with people I considered blind. I could get around in decent light, I could go most anywhere without too much help, and because I was adept at hiding my impairment, I appeared ridiculously normal, especially at St. Paul's.

I hung a few things on wire hangers behind an old paisley cloth that was unhemmed and coming apart on the sides. I slid my listening equipment under the bed and went downstairs. The lobby had been cleared of visitors. It was depressing, this checkered linoleum floor with four rows of chrome and vinyl chairs, a standing ashtray at the end of each row. It had become the domain of the blind.

No one was talking. Three women sat in one row, one or two empty chairs between each of them, and several men, equally separated, slumped sadly two rows away. I thought of a desolate Hopper painting of a waiting room in some Greyhound station at three in the morning.

The place was so strange that I was at a loss as to how to start a conversation. "Have you been here before?" or "Nice day, isn't it?" Would they even know how nice the day was? I mean, really know.

I saw a long-legged young woman. "My name is Andy Potok," I said. I had wanted to say: "What's a pretty girl like you doing in a place like this?"

She turned to face me, almost in my direction, eager to engage, smiling. I saw darkness around her eyes. "Margie Dawson's mine," she said.

"Are you blind?" I heard myself asking. I felt really stupid.

"Yes, I am," Margie said.

"But you're...you're..." I stopped myself from blurting that she was too lovely. "You're so young," I said.

She had an apple-pie prettiness, spoiled only by the puffiness around her eyes. She had a pert button nose, a heart-shaped mouth, an oval face with cascading blond locks.

"I can just see light with one eye, a little movement with the other," she said.

"Jesus," I said. "How did it happen?"

"I'm a diabetic," Margie said. Her eyes were half closed, sometimes opening wide, though with effort; sometimes closing gently, like a bird folding its wings. The flesh under her eyes was blue or purple or gray. "What about you?" she asked.

"I have retinitis pigmentosa," I said. I think she hadn't heard of it. She waited politely for an explanation, and her eyes fluttered, as if to say, "How nice...how nice to meet you...."

She was her disease and I was mine. Diabetic retinopathy meets retinitis pigmentosa.

"What do you do?" Margie asked. "I mean what *did* you do? You are blind, aren't you?"

"I was a painter...a picture painter...."

"Really?" Margie said. "I illustrated greeting cards."

Her smile kept vanishing, too suddenly, draining her face of expression; then just as suddenly it reappeared, her eyes darting left, right, up, down. The effort to look interested and attractive seemed too much for her. It seemed to unlink her features, like a puppet with tangled strings.

Margie told me how diabetes had made her blind, hemorrhages exploding inside her retinas, eventually leaving little but scar tissue. Margie had had a series of operations attempting to seal, weld, sew, scorch, and freeze the tiny delicate webs in the back of her eyes. The operations didn't work, but the surgeons kept trying. She would have another while we were at St. Paul's and a final one after.

More than half of our group was diabetic, and the scope of their problems dwarfed mine. I felt lucky to be only going blind. The diabetics had their terrible frailty to deal with, replacing twice daily the insulin their bodies had stopped producing, watching over their fragile limbs and eyes and vital organs, their constantly threatened lives.

I moved around in the row with the women. It was apparent that I was physically better off than anyone there. Many eyes here were disfigured, with eyeballs bulging, puffed with swelling, darkened and lined by surgery, eyes turned in opposite directions, or fixed in benign, lifeless stares, some open, some closed, some covered with a milky film, some gone altogether. I felt healthy. My eyes were bothersome, irritated, somewhat disturbed, but they were the eyes, suddenly, of a sighted, not a blind, man.

I began to move from row to row, speaking with the

men and the women. I felt so slow-moving at home and so speedy here. Soon everyone was drawn in. We couldn't contain all we had stored for so long. We were finally with people who understood.

"I could see perfectly well until a month ago," Rosemary said. "I was so afraid to come here."

"Kee-rist," said Ray. "I sure didn't want to leave my wife and baby for four goddamn months, but I've got to get myself ready for a new job."

"It's been hell at home," Tommy said. He had an enormous bull neck, and his eyes looked barely attached to his skull. They bulged in opposite directions. He said he was disfigured because of steroid injections meant to help his eyes. "I can't stand just sitting around doing nothing," he said in a lovely Irish tenor. "Boy, am I ever ready to go back to work. That's why I'm here too."

Our voices rose in pitch and loudness. Most of the people who had already gone to bed, swearing that they would never come down, never join in, swearing they would leave this weird place first thing in the morning, now started to straggle down the stairs in bathrobes or T-shirts. Soon we were emptying our clogged hearts of the terrible burdens we hadn't been able to share with anyone.

Margie couldn't stop smiling. "We're all going to be part of things again," she said.

"My mother didn't want to let me out of the goddamn house," Hank said. He had a fancy little tape recorder playing Mantovani into his ear. "She'd want me to just sit there. 'You'll hurt yourself, Hank'—that's all she ever said. Christ."

Betty and Norma, Fred and Hank were all twenty or younger. They seemed to wear their sexuality on the surface, swaggering, boasting, provoking, wrapped tightly in their double-knits, doused with skin bracers and colognes and pimple creams, suffering the pain of an exploded adolescence. Had it not been for their blindness, they probably would have been revving up their twin carburetors at that very moment, leaving black rubber tire tracks in the streets of Providence or Arlington or Fall River.

"Yeah," Betty said. "Just because we can't see doesn't mean we're not normal. You know what I mean?" She turned and muffled a laugh with her arm.

A very large, older man, also named Fred—we dubbed him Big Fred, the other, Little Fred—told us pathetic stories of his family. "They don't know how to say nothin' to me no more. They don't know what to say to a blind man." Herman and Norma recognized the problem and nodded. "And the kids on the block call me 'the blind Greek.' Jesus, I don't like that."

Dot roared with laughter as we told stories of our clumsiness, of banging into everything, feeling one another's newest bruises, shattered calves, scarred foreheads. "Open doors get me," Dot said. "They just come right out of nowhere."

"Kids' shoes," Kathleen added.

"Stairs, stairs going down," I said.

"Yeah," a chorus of voices agreed.

"Fire hydrants."

"Dogs."

"Low branches."

We complained for hours—about talking to an empty chair when someone leaves the room without warning, about being dragged across streets against our will by well-meaning people wanting to help; about being yelled at because we're presumed deaf as well as blind.

We were a bedraggled, motley crew, the fifteen of us, grotesque and fascinating. I felt more comfortable that first evening at St. Paul's than I had felt for a long time, even at home. I belonged here, and I began to love *my* group. I swore that I'd do anything in the world for any of them. They were *my* people.

I couldn't sleep for hours the first night. I had met my blind demons and they were Dot and Tommy and Ray and Margie. I felt the thrill of beginning love affairs. I wanted to protect them all with my superior vision. As everyone snored in our narrow, squalid space, the women on the other side of a thick fire door wired to an alarm, I thought of their wrecked lives, for the first time in a long time not thinking about my own.

I tried to fall asleep with music, which I always carried on buses and trains, even on the shortest trips. I felt that my music defined me, reminded me, even at lost, unhinged times, of my identity. Above all, I kept my Beethoven quartets near me, and now I tried to fall asleep on the back of a lilting section of the C-sharp-minor Quartet. Images of Tommy's left eye wouldn't leave me. In the loud snores of my dorm mates I interpreted diabetic pathologies no internist had ever dreamed of; with my new friends' tossing and turning, I feared the last spasms of hypoglycemic convulsions. I awoke later during that first night to hear only the spinning of my empty tape reel, and when I shut it off, all was quiet.

Martha Weinman Lear

He awoke at 7 A.M. with pain in his chest. The sort of pain that might cause panic if one were not a doctor, as he was, and did not know, as he knew, that it was heartburn.

He went into the kitchen to get some Coke, whose secret syrups often relieve heartburn. The refrigerator door seemed heavy, and he noted that he was having trouble unscrewing the bottle cap. Finally he wrenched it off, cursing the defective cap. He poured some liquid, took a sip. The pain did not go away. Another sip; still no relief.

Now he grew more attentive. He stood motionless, observing symptoms. His breath was coming hard. He felt faint. He was sweating, though the August morning was still cool. He put fingers to his pulse. It was rapid and weak. A powerful burning sensation was beginning to spread through his chest, radiating upward into his throat. Into his arm? No. But the pain was growing worse. Now it was crushing—"*crushing*," just as it is always described. And worse even than the pain was the sensation of losing all power, a terrifying seepage of strength. He could feel the entire degenerative process accelerating. He was growing fainter, faster. The pulse was growing weaker, faster. He was sweating much more profusely now—a heavy, clammy sweat. He felt that the life juices were draining from his body. He felt that he was about to die.

On some level he stood aside and observed all this with a certain clinical detachment. Here, the preposterous spectacle of this thin naked man holding a tumbler of Coke and waiting to die in an orange Formica kitchen on a sunny summer morning in the fifty-third year of his life.

I'll be damned, he thought. I can't believe it.

It had crept up on him so sneakily. He had awakened earlier, at 6:30, with an ache, not a pain really, high up there in the pit of the stomach, and wondering what might have caused it, possibly the broiled-chicken snack at midnight, he had padded into the bathroom and had caught his reflection in the mirror; pallid under the tan, blue eyes dulled, the hollows beneath them deep and dark.

You look like hell, he had told himself. Go back to sleep. It's Saturday.

So he had gone back to bed, but not to sleep. It was a habit he could not break. Whether he had slept eight hours or two, alone or not, in his own bed or in some vacation spot five thousand miles from home; whether he had worked or boozed or counted his debts or fought with his wife or mourned a friend the night before; on weekends or on New Year's Day, with or without headaches, backaches, upper respiratories, whatever: even when he willed himself to linger in the bed and there was no reason at all not to do so, he was always up at 6:30, his own most reliable alarm clock, instantly alert, ready to wash, dress, gulp the coffee, scan the front page, drive to the hospital and appear at 8 A.M. in the operating room, scrubbed and ready to cut. A habit.

He had lain there thinking about this habit, and perhaps finally he had dozed for a few minutes, but then he had wakened again with the pain worse, and had gone for the Coke. And now he was at the edge of an abyss.

He made his way back to the bedroom, clutching walls for support. He eased himself onto the bed, picked up the telephone receiver and, with fingers that felt like foreign objects, dialed the Manhattan emergency number.

A woman's voice, twangy: "This is 911. Can I help you?"

He spoke slowly, struggling to enunciate each word clearly:

"My name is Dr. Harold Lear. I live at_____. I am, having a heart attack. My doctor's name is_____. I am too weak to look up his number. Please call him and tell him to come right away."

"Sir, I'm sorry. This is 911. I can't call your doctor."

"But I need him."

"Well, I'm sorry. This is *strictly* an *emergency service*."

"This is an emergency. A heart attack."

"Sir, I'm very sorry." Reproach in the voice. "I *can't* call your doctor. We don't *do* that."

He thought he might laugh or cry. He felt trapped in an old Nichols and May routine: I think my arm is broken. Yes, sir, what is your Blue Cross number? I don't know. You don't *know*? Well, I don't have my card, but I have this arm, you see. . . . You don't *have your card*? You should *always* carry your card. . . .

Now he felt not panic, but a certain professional urgency. A familiar statistic plucked at his brain like an advertising slogan: 50 percent of all coronary victims die in the first ten minutes. "Thank you," he said to 911, and hung up.

Slowly he tugged on a robe, staggered back into the

foyer and pressed for the elevator. At this hour it was on self-service. When it arrived, he entered, pushed 1 and CLOSE DOOR, and braced himself against the wall. Suddenly he knew that if he did not lie down he would fall. He lowered himself to the floor. When the elevator door opened, he rolled out into the lobby and said to the startled doorman, "Get a wheelchair. Get me to the emergency room. I am having a heart attack."

"An ambulance, Doctor? Shouldn't we get an ambulance?"

"No. No time. A wheelchair." Then he lost clarity.

He was next aware of being in a wheelchair that was careening down the street. His head was way back, resting against a softness that seemed to be a belly. He did not know whose it was, but he was so pleased to have that belly for support.

The hospital—his hospital, where he was on staff—was nearby, a few blocks from his home. He felt the wheelchair take a corner with a wild side-to-side lurch and go rattling on toward the emergency room. Though his mind was floating and he could not keep his eyes open, that curiously disengaged observer within him reached automatically for the pulse. He could no longer detect any beat. He was very cold, very clammy, and he knew that he was in shock.

I am dying now, he thought. I am dying in a creaky wheelchair that is rattling down the avenue, half a block from the emergency room. Isn't this *silly*. And then: Well, if I am dying, why isn't my life flashing in front of me? Nothing is flashing. Where is my life?

The apartment-house doorman, who was steering the wheelchair, and a janitor, who was running alongside, recalled later that he was smiling. They wondered why.

Finally the chair screeched to a halt. He opened his eyes. Crutches, pulleys, traction, all the paraphernalia of an orthopedic treatment room. Damn it, he thought, we've come to the wrong place. A uniformed security guard stood nearby, eyeing him idly. "Excuse me," he said to the guard, "but I am having a heart attack. Can you direct us to the right room?" And slipped out of consciousness again.

Then, dimly, he felt himself being lifted onto a stretcher, sensed noise and light and a sudden commotion about him. They were giving him nasal oxygen, taking his pulse, taking his blood pressure, starting an intravenous, getting a cardiogram—the total force of modern emergency care suddenly mobilized; a team clicking away with the impersonality of an overwhelmingly efficient machine.

He understood that at this moment he was no more than a body with pathology. They were not treating a person; they were treating an acute coronary case in severe shock. They were racing, very quickly, against time. He himself had run this race so often, working in just this detached silent way on nameless, faceless bodies with pathologies. He did not resent the impersonality. He simply noted it. But one of the medical team, a young woman who was taking his blood pressure, seemed concerned about him. She patted him on the shoulder. She said, "How do you feel?" It was the only departure from this cool efficiency, and he felt achingly grateful for it. Ah, he thought in some fogged corner of the brain, she must be a medical student. She hasn't yet learned to depersonalize. She will. We all do. What a pity.

(Later—he thought it was that same day, but it may have been the next—she came up to the coronary-care unit, and took his hand and said, "How are you doing,

Dr. Lear?" and smiled at him. He never knew her name, and he never forgot her.)

The painkillers had taken effect now. He could breathe. A whitecoated figure said, "Well, there's no question about your having a heart attack."

What a dumb way to put it, he thought. I don't know what he's saying, "What do you mean, 'no question'? Did I or didn't I?"

"You *did. Look.*" The doctor, clearly irritated, thrust the cardiogram reading in front of his face. He peered at it. The fine ink lines traced a crazy path across the paper tape. Groggy as he was, he could see that he was having one hell of a heart attack.

Now administrative forces descended upon him. They asked about next-of-kin.

His wife was out of the country, he said.

Where?

He wasn't sure.

Children?

His son was traveling too. He could not remember his daughter's married name.

Siblings? None. Parents? None. Finally he gave them the name of a friend.

His own doctor was abroad. The covering doctor was a stranger to him. "Whom do you want?" they asked. He couldn't think of anyone else. This seemed to rattle them. He could not simply be admitted; he had to have an admitting doctor. They conferred for what seemed like a very long time while he lay there, feeling agreeably hazy, bittersweet strains of Nichols and May playing again in his ear. Finally they sent him upstairs, doctorless.

He remembered thinking, just before he passed into a long, deep sleep, How can I get hold of Martha? I've

got to get hold of Martha, because if I die without telling her, she will never forgive me.

He knew this was the logic of a deranged mind. A
nurse wondered, as his street escorts had wondered
earlier, why he was smiling.

II

From *The Long Walk Home*
Leonard Kriegel

But as soon as I was back in the chair, the world was mine once again, and I swallowed my fear and hate. I really loved the chair then. The threat of my fitting made the love even more open, and I looked upon the chair now as if it really were the thread of my survival. But I had to show it, to myself and to others. For the next few weeks all I could think of was some dramatic way, a moment of truth, in which I could show the world my latest posture. But it was Willie who thought of it for me.

Willie possessed the gambler's instinct. Even today, when I comb him out of my memory, I see him as our ward's hunch player, as ready as George Raft to ride his instinct all the way. And, somehow, he was always uncovering ideas I had searched for. It was hard to take. After each idea, I had to cut another notch in the belt of his Irish *mazel*. But, to his credit, he sometimes looked to me to play the prince to his Machiavelli. He could surrender his ideas with effortless grace, playing clown or adjutant to my generalship.

It was an early September morning, about three weeks after my fitting, and the two of us were on our way back to the ward from nine o'clock therapy sessions. By this time, both Willie and I were wearing braces. But we rarely walked on them, except for the half-hour lesson in walking that we now had each afternoon. Willie got the idea from the last week's movie, a western with the inevitable cavalry charge at the end. And that made it even worse, because as soon as he told it to me, I knew that I should have thought of it myself.

"Well," he asked, as we turned into the short corridor leading to the elevator, "you for it?"

"For it! Willie, you're a genius. You're smarter than every goddamn doctor in this place. For Christ's sake, you're smarter than...than Einstein."

Willie giggled and slammed his chair into the elevator door, a habit of his, another token of defiance for the world. We sat there, filled with this newest excitement, waiting for the elevator. Even when the elevator door opened and I saw that John was running it, my happiness didn't leave. And I felt even better than Willie, who somehow could show his contempt for John and get away with it, said, "What took ya so long?"

"Don't get fresh with me, you dumb Mick son of a bitch," John said. But it was hollow, as if he were afraid of Willie.

When the elevator stopped, we backed our chairs out. Then Willie winked at me and, turning to John, said, "Listen, John, ya know what Lennie and me are goin' to do? We're goin' to have our own invasion...like Normandy last year."

"You're crazy," John said, not even smiling. "You're crazy like all Micks."

Willie laughed. "Who's crazy? If you were in a chair, John, maybe we'd let ya come."

"Crazy Mick bastard," John snorted. And with that, he slammed the door and disappeared.

We pushed down the corridor into the ward. Then we wheeled into the back room, where we joined Natey and a boy named Steve Drago who had arrived at the Rock a month after me. "The thing is," Willie said, ignoring their presence, "if they catch us, they'll really give it to us." He burrowed his right fist into the palm of his left hand. "Like that. I want ya to be ready. They may even take away our chairs."

"To hell with what they'll take away," I said. "Anyway, how're they going to find out? They'll never suspect anything. Look, we can do it tonight."

"Tonight?" Willie said.

"What're you talking about?" Natey asked.

"Yeah, tonight," I said, ignoring Natey. "Right after supper."

"Listen, what're you talking about?" Natey insisted.

"Shall we tell him?" Willie asked.

"Okay," I said. "But keep your mouth shut, Natey. And you too, Steve."

We told them, and they were both eager to join. Then the four of us began talking about who else might want to go, and I suggested that we toss it open for anyone in a chair. By this time, I had assumed my generalship, a right that the others silently acknowledged. What I wanted was an alliance of equals, a revolution with style. And so I had to restrict the invasion to those of us in wheel chairs. I knew that it was going to be hard on the boys we called the "Birds"—on Lobashevski, on Luigi, on Jerry Levine, all of whom had their arms encased in braces—but I was already in love with the memory of that cavalry charge. And how stupid it would have looked for Luigi or Lobashevski or Jerry to follow us with their arms hooked up to those braces. Chicken wings, we called them. I wanted lions, not eagles. And even though I felt that I was betraying the birds, I excused myself with the thought that such were the responsibilities of leadership.

The word spread, and by lunchtime almost *every*

wheelchair patient in the ward had joined our expedition. In the afternoon, while I sat in my cubicle, planning the expedition, Lobashevski came over. Before he could even say anything, I announced, in my most abrupt military manner, "You can't come. It's only for rollers. No birds."

Ever since I had arrived in Ward B, Lobashevski had courted me. Still, he gave me the "Who died and left you king?" line.

I was intent on being nice, partially to soothe his feelings and partially to soothe my own ruffled conscience. "You just can't come, Tommy. It's nothing pesonal. It's just that the plan is only for guys in chairs. None of the birds are coming."

"What're you going to do if I squeal?"

"I'll break your skinny neck, that's what I'll do."

Lobashevski swallowed. Then he bit into his lower lip and I knew that I had him. Tears filled his eyes, but he didn't cry. I wanted to say something that would make him feel better, but I couldn't think of anything, and so I shut up as he walked away.

After supper, we left the back room in groups of twos and threes, having arranged to meet at the gate to the Garnerville road. I stayed behind, signaling the moment of departure (the signal was palms spread out, a baseball umpire's *safe* call) for each group. The first group consisted of Burp Burp, Jackie Spolino, and Natey, who were to go up the hill, as if they were going to visit the girls' ward, and then circle around the Rock until they came to the Garnerville gate. On summer evenings, we were permitted the run of the Home's grounds until nine o'clock. I had stationed Willie on the porch right outside the nurse's office to see when Miss Logan wasn't in the office. Miss Logan was seldom in her office; she preferred the ward for younger children just across the hall. There was no trouble getting the others down the ramp. Finally I wheeled up to Willie, and the two of us went down the ramp and headed for the gate.

When we reached the gate, the others were all there. Natey pounded me happily on the back, and Kenneth Olensky insisted on shaking my hand. But, general that I was, I received their adulation with a minimum of embarrassment and a sigh of emotional trial. A battle, I remembered, was not a war. I looked at Natey's watch (Natey was one of the few boys in the ward who had a watch), creasing my brow with brash Hollywood-soldier consciousness. It was twenty after six.

"Well, Lennie," Jackie Spolino said, drumming his fingers on the rims of his wheels, "it should be easy from here on."

"Remember to stay organized," I ordered, ignoring Jackie. "That's the most important thing."

"You're the leader, Lennie," Burp Burp announced. "Anything you say, that's what goes."

We have to be back a quarter to eight. . .eight the latest," I said. "I figure it'll take us fifteen or twenty minutes each way. That leaves us with about three quarters of an hour in Garnerville."

"What'll we do when we get there?" someone asked from the rear of the circle that had gathered around me.

"What's the difference?" Natey said. "As long as we get there."

"I figured that out, too," I said. Ever since I had come to the Home, I had been curious about Garnerville, and I had spoken about it to some of the stretcher-bearers who lived there and who worked in the Rock during the summer. In the winter, some of them hung out in a candy store a few doors to the left at the bottom of the hill that led into the town. "We'll go down the hill in formation. Line up across the road. I'll be in front. When you hear Willie sound the charge, you follow me down. Willie, you remember the signal?" Willie nodded. "At the bottom, we stop and line up in twos. There's a candy store a few doors to the left. That's where we're going."

"What about cars?" Kenneth Olensky asked.

"To hell with cars," Willie said.

I turned my chair around, waved my hand in the air, and began to move. "Let's go," I called.

It was easy going, except where the road curved and where it got narrow. I had timed it well enough. When we came to the top of the hill, I called Natey over and took a look at his watch. It was almost twenty to seven. I really felt like a general then. "Halt!" I cried. I looked down the hill. The road was wide enough at the top, but it grew narrower, especially at the bottom where we needed room enough to make the turn. I called Willie over.

"What's the matter?" Kenneth Olensky called.

"Shut up!" Willie answered.

Willie and I huddled together, furtively whispering, while Willie, loyal to his training at the Rock, occasionally glanced over his shoulder. We decided to change the plan and break up into two waves of six each because of the narrowness of the hill at the bottom. Willie was to command the second wave. "But what about the bugle?" I remembered.

"I can be the bugle and commander of the second wave, too," Willie said.

We lined the chairs up, making sure that there was enough room between each one. Then I wheeled to the front of my wave. Just before I raised my hand in the air to signal the charge, I noticed that the front yards of the houses facing the road contained chickens. Christ, I thought, it's real country. Then I remembered that I hated chickens and I dropped my hand, hearing Willie's rather hoarse imitation of a bugle as I began down the hill.

Bent low in the chair, my hand loosely fingering the wheel rims, I felt as if I were falling into something deep. And I wanted so much to fall, because falling struck me then as the most beautiful of all possibilities. The wind seemed to fold against my body, as if space were opening for me alone. As I went rapidly past one of the houses, I caught a glimpse of an old woman standing on the porch, her face vapid with terror and disbelief. When I hit the bottom of the hill, I took the turn fast and clean, spinning rapidly around to come to a sudden halt after I had gone around twenty feet into the street. When I turned, I saw Willie take the turn, leaning over to his left, just enough to tilt the chair slightly and take it on two wheels. I envied Willie his style, but I was much too happy with myself to feel that for more than a second.

The candy store was just five doors down. It didn't look like any of the candy stores I had known in the city, no black and white tile on the outside, not even a Coke sign overhead. It was no more than a red-brick front on a shingle house; the only sign, a small neon one in the dusty window, read "Ice Cream Sold Here." The country, I thought. What can you expect?

Willie wheeled over to me. "Look at them," he said, pointing at three or four people gathered in a group across the street and staring at us. "They're scared. They're scared shitless."

I pointed to the door. "Let's go inside," I said.

Just then, a man of about forty-five, with a body that seemed to be all stomach, and wearing a dirty white apron, appeared in the doorway. He reminded me of Schrager (who, by the way, was the only wheel-chair patient in the ward who hadn't joined us), and even

before he said, "You can't come in here, boys," I dislik-
ed him.

"Who're you?" Willie asked, puzzled. He was on my
right, the other chairs drawn up in a semicircle, two
deep, around us.

"Keep quiet, Willie," I said. It was the first test of my
generalship, and I decided to try to appeal to his
"We're just a group of poor unfortunates" side. "Look,
mister," I said meekly, "all we want to do is buy some
things. Soda and candy and stuff. That's all."

"Sorry," he said, his voice rheumy and irritating, "I
can't let you in."

"But mister," I said, emphasizing *mister*, "that's all
we want. We're not going to mess up your place. We
have money." I removed a dollar bill from my wallet
and held it up for him to see.

"I'm sorry," he said. "I'm really sorry for you boys.
But I can't let you in and that's all there is to it." He
stared over my head while he spoke, and I turned my
head to look at the group across the street. There were
around ten of them now. A few pointing in our direction, shaking their heads while they spoke. Then a big,
muscular man, wearing a gray shirt and gray slacks,
broke out of their midst and began to trot across the
street. His badge told me who he was, and I swallowed, the serpent in my soul laughing at my fear.

"What's the matter, Dave?" the law asked as he
stepped onto the curbstone.

"There's nothing the matter," Natey said loudly.

"Nothing," Burp Burp repeated, sententiously shaking his head. "Nothing."

"Look, sir," I said, this time emphasizing *sir*, "all we
want to do is buy some stuff. Then he goes and blocks
the entrance."

"They're sick, Mike," Fat Boy replied. "How can I let them in? I got customers to think of. And they got germs."

"We haven't got a goddamn thing," Willie said disgustedly. By this time, Willie was very angry. His hands were bloodless white from clenching the wheel rims.

"What's wrong with you boys?" the law asked, looking at me.

"We haven't got germs," I answered. "Do you think they'd let us out with germs?"

My logic had him. He nodded. "Then what's wrong with you?" he repeated.

"We had polio...most of us, anyhow." At this, he simply stared at me.

"Infantile paralysis," Natey said.

Now he smiled with understanding. He nodded. "You're not contagious then?"

"Of course not," Willie said, as if he had just been insulted.

"Sir," I said, "we haven't had any germs for a long time. Polio is contagious for about a week...maybe ten days at most. That's when they put you in isolation." He was nodding again, impressed, I imagined, by my lucidity. "Most of us," I added triumphantly, "have had it for at least a year."

"And they don't send you up the hill," Burp Burp shouted, pointing in the direction of the Rock, "until you ain't contagious any more."

The law waved to the group across the street to tell them that they could come over now. But none of them moved. Then he frowned and mumbled something I didn't catch. Turning to me again, he asked, "How'd you get here?"

I didn't want to answer. But I knew that I had to. And I wasn't going to lie. "We just wheeled down," I said, evading his eyes.

"Did you get permission?"

"We didn't ask."

He stared at me for a few seconds. Then he scanned our group. Finally he turned to Fat Boy, who was still blocking the entrance. "Let them in, Dave."

"But, Mike," Fat Boy protested, "they're sick. Look I don't want to hurt their feelings. But I got my customers to think about."

"Up yours, Mac," Willie mumbled under his breath.

"Do me a favor, Dave," the law repeated. "Let them in. They're not sick."

Fat Boy hesitated. Then he shrugged his shoulders, turned, and went back inside the store. We had won. And winning was a good feeling, a very good feeling, even though I didn't want any of his soda or any of his other stuff by now. "Thanks," I said, turning to the law.

"It's okay." He placed his hands on the back of my chair, the largest hands I had ever seen. "But you be sure to get back before they miss you. Don't stay too long."

There was a low step at the entrance, but the law picked the back wheels of each chair up for us. The store was much too narrow for twelve wheel chairs, and once inside I was ready to go back out again. But I stayed and bought a few baseball cards. The chewing gum that came with the cards I threw away. That was all that I bought. But most of the others, destitute of self-control, inflicted their contempt on Fat Boy by feeding him money. It angered me, especially when I had to lend Willie a quarter. Willie should have known better.

We must have been in the store for twenty minutes, long enough and noisy enough to have made Fat Boy wish we would get the hell out—and long enough to make him richer, too. When we left, I gathered the chairs together right outside the door. Fat Boy followed us to the doorway, his face pale with the relief of the victim who thinks he may have escaped and yet isn't sure. Only a few people were across the street now; more than half the crowd had gone, although those that remained were still staring at us, like wax dolls molded in the supreme moment of doubt. I still don't understand it. They allowed their children to work in the wards.

"Good-by, you hicks," Willie shouted happily. "And up yours," he added, turning in his chair to Fat Boy.

But Fat Boy didn't answer him. He just remained in the doorway, looking at us. Then he turned and walked back inside, carefully closing the door behind him. "Okay," I shouted, so that people across the street could hear me. "Line up the same way to go back. Same five guys with me. Rest with Willie." The chairs scrambled into position. I stared at the people across the street. You bastards, I thought, and spit over the side of my chair. A middle-aged woman skipped a step backwards when I spit. We could see her face flush with embarrassment even from across the street. Willie's giggle was followed by Burp Burp's shrill, staccato laughter. It was then that I realized how tense we all were. I waved. "Let's go."

Going up the hill was easy enough. But we were very quiet now. All the way back to the ward we were quiet. Someone, I think it was Jackie Spolino, began to sing but quickly dropped it when no one else picked the song up. It was as if, already on the way back, we were storing it in the memory, to re-enact our defiance during the dead winter days when the snow on the ground kept us confined to the ward and the Rock. The serpent wasn't laughing any more either, for I was no longer worried about getting caught. What could they do to us? Take away our wheel-chair "privileges" and keep us from the next movie. Or Major Wilson, that shriveled soul the Governor had recently appointed as Director of the Home—Major Wilson might gather us together in the auditorium, there to puncture our freedom by wailing about how we had, with our "undisciplined behavior," given the New York State Reconstruction Home a "bad name" with the "good people of Garnerville." But to hell with him, too. He couldn't take away our victory over Fat Boy.

I wasn't really surprised to see Miss Logan waiting for us at the foot of the ramp, looking as if she wanted to do nothing so much as to beat the living Jesus out of us. But she didn't say anything. She pursed her mouth and herded us up onto the porch and then led us into the back room. She pointed to the door leading to the ward, and I pushed myself through first. And I suppose that was the sweetest moment of the evening. For all of the birds and the others who had remained behind began to whistle and clap. Even Lobashevski was whistling. And Schrager, too. That really got me. Miss Logan's pursed mouth just dropped and for a few moments she was too stunned to say anything. Then, the thin veins of her neck standing out like steel bands, she shouted, "Quiet! Do you hear me? Quiet!" The clapping and whistling stopped, but everyone was smiling. Miss Logan ordered us to bed, even though it was only twenty to eight. But that was all. She just waited until we were in bed, switched the lights off, and left the ward.

The following day, after supper, Natey and I wheeled down to the auditorium. We went into the john and remained there, each of us puffing away on cigarettes Natey had bummed from one of the Garnerville stretcher-bearers.

"Willie wants to do it again," Natey said. "He wants you to lead us tomorrow night."

"No," I said. "This one's enough. Maybe next summer."

"I guess you're right." He blew what he called a smoke ring, and the two of us watched it evaporate into the ceiling. "Jesus, it was good. Wasn't it good?"

"Yeah," I answered. But I was feeling tired and somewhat depressed; I didn't really want to talk about what we had done.

"You know what I'd want to do though?"

"What?"

"I'd like to go down 9W. Past Haverstraw and past the town after that. And I'd like to keep going until I got to the bridge."

"And then what would you do?"

"Well, I'd go halfway across. And then I'd stop. I'd wait until there were a lot of people watching. And then...." He paused to drag on the cigarette, then smiled. "Then I'd spit into the Hudson."

The wheel chair was the way home.

From *Face to Face*
Ved Mehta

I was in the States. In my imagination the land appeared as boundless, as infinite as the oceans themselves, and I longed for an impression, any impression, which in years to come I should be able to remember. At home one could hardly go half a mile straight—there were curves, turns, alleys and back streets, and with the windows of the car rolled down, you could hear the rhythmic tread of a horse harnessed to a *tonga*, the occasional cracking of the whip of the *tonga* man as he tried to get his clients quickly to their destinations. There were the tinkling bells of the bicycles and the curses of the ever-present bicycle riders, who swore at the *tonga* men for blocking their way, and the sepoys, who cursed the bicycle men for cursing and blew whistles at the *tonga* men at every corner for going so fast. Yes, the streets I remembered in India were streets of unmistakable life, with colourful sounds and profane language, with bends and turns. But the street that I was now riding on seemed to stretch before me wide and straight, and it was quiet. The taxi driver had not yet used his horn and carried on no conversations with his fellow drivers. In these streets, I thought, you could travel fast and you could always get places, and smoothly, too.

On my right in the back seat sat Mrs. DeFranco, saying, "Oh, you simply had a dreadful trip, poor boy. What a terrible way to arrive."

"I didn't mind it," I said.

"Oh, but just imagine having all the contents of your bags stolen."

"I have two bags, Mrs. DeFranco," I said, "and one of them is still full."

"I know, but what a bad introduction to America." She took both my hands in hers. Then suddenly she broke into laughter. There was something that seemed open and unrestrained about her laugh. I had heard women laugh in India but never quite that way.

"Why do you laugh?" I asked, baffled.

"I just realized that all this time you've had your hand inside your jacket. Are you afraid of losing your wallet, too?"

"I hadn't meant to," I muttered. I could feel the blood rising in my cheeks.

The taxi driver had joined in the laughter by now and was eagerly awaiting the details of the theft. He was almost as curious as a *tonga* man, I thought to myself, and the muscles of my jaw relaxed. Mrs. DeFranco described to the driver how I had come up to the baggage counter to collect my bags and found that one of them had been broken into, and how we had had to remain at the airport for two hours, filling up forms and cataloguing the articles lost for the insurance people. The driver kept on exclaiming, intermittently, "Oh, too bad. So sorry to hear that. What a bum way to enter the country." I kept on wishing all the while that Mrs. DeFranco would stop. After all, as the baggageman had told me, it was the first robbery from a passenger's bags that he could remember.

But the inquisitive driver persisted. "How did it happen?"

"It seems," I explained, "that someone broke into my bag while it was being taken from the airplane to the terminal."

"Well, it shouldn't have happened to you, sir," the

driver said, and Mrs. DeFranco added, "It shouldn't have happened at all."

I kept waiting for the driver to take a turn. (I remember that when he finally did, it was a sharp right turn, and not the half-bend to which I had been accustomed.) I broke into their conversation, "Where do you live, Mrs. DeFranco?"

"On Broadway," she said.

"Is Broadway a wide street?" I asked.

She laughed. "Oh, it is the centre of the universe."

"No, Times Square is," the driver said.

"But Times Square is on Broadway," Mrs. DeFranco reminded the driver, and laughed again.

The centre of the universe, that's where I was, I thought, a centre of the universe without the circumference which I'd always imagined the universe to have. In India the universe was an endless circle and here it was a horizontal line. I wanted to tell this to my two companions, but I did not know how to begin or how I could make it clear to them.

In India my life had been routine, a circle of routine from which there was no escape. It was like being on a merry-go-round, always in the midst of colourful things but nevertheless circumscribed by the monotonous movement of the merry-go-round. Being in America seemed like being on a swift train, and the life was full, indeed bursting, with incidents, like your bag being broken into.

It was too early to tell which of the two I preferred.

"How was your plane ride otherwise, sir?" asked the inquisitive driver.

"Yes," Mrs. DeFranco said, "tell us about it; it must have been very exciting indeed."

I wondered what I could tell them. Could I tell them

what my father had said just before I boarded the plane?

"You will have to learn not to be so shy and sensitive," he had said. "You'll have to become thick-skinned."

And my sister Umi had remarked in her usually light manner, "Daddyji, you certainly can't expect him to be thick-skinned when he only weighs six and a half stone."

"What do you mean?" I had retorted. "I'm almost five foot five."

Sister Nimi had tried to console me by saying, "He looks like a man. What are you saying, Umi?"

Sitting in the airplane, I had tried very hard to put this conversation from my mind. I said to myself that I was a man. After all, I was almost fifteen and a half; and with my overcoat on, no one could tell how slender my "boyish body" was. That was another of the phrases sister Umi used when she talked about me, and however much I tried to console myself, still the phrase had caught like a thorn in my mind. That first night on the plane I slept a little while, only to dream of a full-sized mirror. For the first time I was seeing my reflection in the mirror, and I was beating it, saying, "I am a man, not a boy, a man."

I jolted awake, breathing hard. I supposed it was morning, although inside the plane it was hard to tell. I'd never been closeted like that before, and the senses of sound, smell and even touch were dulled by the incessant roar of the machine so that to a blind man night and day merged into one. I surmised it was morning, because shortly the air hostess gently tapped my shoulder and said, "Sir, care for some breakfast now?"

My first inclination was to say yes, because my

stomach did feel empty, but in a moment I remembered that my father wasn't there, and how would I eat breakfast? All my life I'd eaten with my hands. A spoon was the only implement I had ever used, and that very rarely. A week before leaving home my father had tried to give me quick lessons in eating with a knife and fork, but I felt as clumsy with them as I would have trying to read Braille with gloves on. The effort required to cut the meat from the bone of a lamb chop was frustrating and terrifying for me.

"Not yet," I said to the hostess, "but I should like some orange juice."

That morning I felt more keenly than ever the need of that support I had left behind me. I had postponed learning to eat with a knife and fork in the hope that I would learn it from my father on the way. Then my father had not been able to come with me.

"Are you on a diet?" the hostess asked me once.

"No," I said. "I am just trying to follow Gandhiji."

"Ah," she said, "but he fasted for twenty-one days, and I understand he didn't even drink orange juice."

"I, too, may have to," I said, and although I said this with a forced smile I took my words more seriously than did the ironic hostess.

"Please don't go on a hunger strike, sir," she said, "against our airline."

"It's not the airline," I said, biting my tongue, "but there are some religious reasons." And by this statement I knew I had raised myself in her estimation, for when we stopped in Brussels she had special flasks of orange juice ordered for me, and I had an ample supply to last me across the Atlantic.

More than once I wished that Mother had let me carry the chocolates in my handbag rather than stuffing them into a laundry bag along with socks and underwear, and then sewing it to my overcoat. "You can carry more with you like this," she said, "for they won't weigh your overcoat."

Often I was on the verge of asking the hostess to bring me my overcoat, but the fear of being shamed because of the laundry bag kept my mouth shut and my stomach empty. I tried to minimize the sensation of hunger as much as possible by blowing up my stomach with frequent glasses of orange juice. The more I thought about the predicament of the knife and fork, which the sensation of hunger never let me forget, and the more I reflected upon my puny size, the more gloomy I became. I despaired at how long I could keep up the pretence and my pride.

I was about to phrase a sentence including the words "pretence" and "pride," describing my trip for the benefit of my two companions in the taxi, when Mrs. DeFranco gently pressed my hand and said, "Poor boy, you still have difficulty with the language, don't you?"

"Yes, it is a language difficulty," I said, belatedly.

The driver remarked, "Sure enough, I have difficulty speaking English. I could never learn to speak Hindu."

"Hindi, you mean," I corrected.

"You see?" he said, with another jolly laugh. Mrs. DeFranco and I joined him, and laughing, we turned on to Broadway.

"Ved, we'll soon be home," Mrs. DeFranco told me, "and then you and my husband can have great fun together. I know you will have a lot in common." He was blind and I was blind and she thought, therefore, that we would of course enjoy one another's company.

"Here we are," the driver said, coming to a stop,

and I hastily pulled out the two dollars an American friend of my mother's had given her and handed it to the driver.

"That won't be enough," Mrs. DeFranco said.

"But it is ten *rupees*!" I said. "One could hire a *tonga* in India for a whole day for that."

"This is America," she said.

"All I have is a cheque for eighty dollars," I said, with embarrassment. Mrs. DeFranco paid the balance, and the taxi driver put both my bags on the curb, shook my hand and said, "If I go to India, I will remember not to become a *tonga* hustler." Then he drove away. Uncertain as to what to do next, I stood there while I heard Mrs. DeFranco click her purse shut. She grabbed the empty bag and asked, "Can you carry the other one?"

"Of course," I said, and lifted it up. Then, with a quick motion, she tucked my hand under her arm and led me to the apartment building. As we climbed the four flights of stairs up to the apartment, I wondered what a woman in India would have done to lead a blind man. She probably would have cringed at such an immediate contact of flesh with a strange man, even as my hand was instinctively pulling away from Mrs. DeFranco's arm. But this thought did not prevent me from being conscious of her well-developed muscles and thinking that America itself, at least, did not hold blind men at arm's length.

Had a bomb exploded in that quiet apartment, I could not have been more surprised than I was when Mr. DeFranco exchanged a loud kiss with his wife upon our entrance. I wondered if my mother would have permitted me to spend my first days in America with the DeFrancos, had she known that my hosts kissed in public.

I was already frightened of Mr. DeFranco. His handshake was firm and masculine, his voice unmistakably that of a trained musician, and the casual way he took my shoulder and led me to the living-room revealed a confidence which I had never known among the blind in India.

"Muriel tells me you have some bad luck," he said, bringing my bags after me into the living room.

"Not bad enough to prevent me from coming," I said.

He laughed. "You were delayed so long that I started preparing your dinner."

"Oh, you cook?" I asked, unable to contain the astonishment I felt.

"Sometimes," he remarked casually, "I help Muriel." He started apologizing for not coming to the airport. "Your arrival time coincided with the lesson of one of my pupils."

"Don't mention it," I said.

"Besides," he continued, "I knew you wouldn't mind being greeted first by a charming lady."

"We had a delightful ride from the airport," I said.

His pacing up and down the living-room was distracting for his footfalls were heavy on the floor.

Mrs. DeFranco asked from the kitchen if I ate meat.

"I do," I said. I had been about to say no, for I did not welcome the ordeal of cutting it, but my hunger got the best of my shame.

She sighed with relief. "John and I have been playing guessing games about it."

"I promised my mother I would gain some weight and my father that I would eat any and everything in America."

"Even beef?" she asked in astonishment, and I mechanically recited the sentence from my grammar book, "When in Rome do as the Romans do."

Then Mrs. DeFranco served the dinner and while she was filling our glasses, she casually remarked, "The peas are at twelve o'clock, the meat balls at six, and spaghetti is in the middle."

"Do you understand that code?" asked Mr. DeFranco.

"No," I said.

"We use the clock dial to locate the food on the plate."

"It is an ingenious way of doing it," Mrs. DeFranco remarked, "and you would hardly find any blind in America who would not understand it. I was sure that blind everywhere knew it."

"Darling, you forget," Mr. DeFranco interrupted, "that India has many primitive conditions, and without a doubt work for the blind there is very backward."

"There is nothing in India," I snapped, "primitive or backward."

The quiet sound of Mr. DeFranco drinking his water stopped, and after a pause he said, "I didn't mean it that way."

"I'm sorry," I said, lifting my water to drink. We began to eat.

I was glad that meat balls did not need to be cut, and during Mrs. DeFranco's trips to the kitchen I took my largest bites of spaghetti. The stubborn peas, which kept sliding off the plate, and my constant wishing Mrs. DeFranco away in the kitchen prevented the conversation at the table from being more than desultory.

My fast, which had lasted forty-eight hours from India to America, had left me weak and dizzy, but the absence of the vigilant airline hostess and the frequent runs to the kitchen by Mrs. DeFranco finally permitted me to fill myself comfortably so that I was ready after dinner to explore the lives of my new acquaintances.

Once we had finished our apple pie and settled into easy-chairs, I asked Mr. DeFranco if he would tell me about himself.

"My life," he began, "is simple and rather unromantic."

"Oh," I persisted, "you are being modest."

"No," he said in a matter-of-fact way. "I spent twelve years at Perkins Institute for the Blind. I entered when I was six, left when I was eighteen. After some college work I came to New York, started giving music lessons and appearing on radio now and then to sing, married Muriel, and here I am."

As he spoke I pictured to myself how similar a life to his I might have had. Dr. Halder had tried to get me to Perkins as early as my seventh birthday. I might very well have studied music there, and then like Mr. DeFranco settled in New York as an accomplished musician, to live by my talents. But marriage?

As it was, he had education, grace and independence, and I had none of these.

"How was your life at Perkins?" I asked, suppressing the awe and envy I felt for him.

"Not too different from that of millions of other kids," he said matter-of-factly. "It was normal and uneventful. We played and studied like all other children."

"What was it really like?" I persisted.

"A great deal of fun," he added absently. "Fun, that's what it was."

I projected into the word "fun" all the imagined qualities that I attributed to his life. But I did not want him to say any more about his life at Perkins, because I had a vague feeling he might spoil it for me.

"Now that you know all about me," he said, "tell me about yourself."

"Yes, do," Mrs. DeFranco added. "We have heard so much about India. It must be a very exciting place."

While I was silently wondering whether my hosts would be interested in the Panditji, my music teacher, the division of India, or Ram Saran's comment on Partition—"it was all in the cards"—Mrs. DeFranco asked if I would mind very much if she finished the dishes.

"Not at all," I said. "I am rather tired now, but perhaps some day we can have a long talk about my past in India."

"Soon, I hope," she said, touching me on my knee, and added with a smile which I could hear, "Don't worry, your English will improve very rapidly." And then in a moment from the kitchen I could hear the plates clattering as Mrs. DeFranco washed them swiftly.

No matter how tired I felt, I knew I could not go to sleep until I had the answer to one more question from Mr. DeFranco. "How did you happen to get married like this?" I asked bluntly.

"What do you mean?" he said laughingly.

"I mean how did it come about? How did you meet her?"

"Very simple," he said. "When I came to New York, she was living in the same apartment house that I was. We met at the door coming and going, I asked her out one night and we came to know each other better, and there you are."

"Just like that?" I asked, for my curiosity was barely whetted.

"Of course," he said.

"Incredible," I could not resist adding.

Only a week before coming to the States I had sat with my father in New Delhi and we had talked about marriage. His manner was candid, his tone serious and compassionate.

"You are old enough so that whether you want it or not, you will think about marriage. You will, of course, not get married for some years, but you will start thinking about it."

"I won't," I said determinedly.

"Don't be shy—it is biological. I wanted to talk with you about this now, as I don't know how long you will be away from home, or when I will see you again."

I waited, all the time thinking about the sea voyage we had planned together. I was sad for him and for me, because the views which he might have imparted to me in two or three weeks had now to be squeezed into the drab hours late in the night.

"My thoughts are wandering," he said, fumbling for words. "You think you might marry a Westerner?" he asked dryly.

"Of course not!" I said emphatically, overcoming the initial shock of the question.

"I have seen a lot of Anglo-Indians," he continued, the pace of his speech increasing, "Anglo-Indians who are fathered by some nameless Englishman and have for their mother some poor Indian. You know what their condition is like?"

But he did not pause for an answer.

"They are ashamed of their mothers because they are black women. These exalted Anglo-Indian children consider themselves white, and superior to their Indian mothers. They have the audacity to speak of England as home. They speak of a country they will never see as their home. Home, indeed!" he said contemptuously.

"The truth is they have no home, no land they can call their own, no father who will own them and no mother whom they will respect. I—I would remain a bachelor, before I would father such a lot." He added reflectively, "In India, at least.

"It hurts me to say this," he continued, with his voice

returning to its normal pitch, "because the irony is that I believe in one world, and I have never believed in the nonsense of superiority of nationalities and races."

There was a calm, fertile moment of communication which I did not choose to break with any response.

"Remember," he went on slowly, "I am speaking of the most degenerate of the Anglo-Indians. They are to be pitied rather than condemned, and again do not forget there are exceptions upon exceptions who do become assimilated into our society.

"There is more than a mere connexion between what I have been saying about the Anglo-Indians and what everyone has been saying about your becoming a misfit in both India and America because of your leaving home so young. Fifteen is a young, a very young, age to be going away."

He paused, and the straining silence was enough to emphasize the danger and gravity of the situation.

"Marriage," he began again, "is, I believe, crucial to a full and rich life, and perhaps even more so in your case. I am fifty-five—an old age for India," and then slowly he repeated, "a very old age. So far you have lived through the eyes of our family. But your leaving home now, my death and the marriage of your sisters and brothers will change it all. Neither your mother and father nor your sisters and brothers can be there all your life to help you live it fully.

"I can never hope to marry you in India well. I am going to be cruel and realistic. To marry you in India would be like trying to marry your sister without her face. I bring this terrifying image to mind because I want you to understand fully how important people think eyes are in any kind of sexual relationship. Men and women fall in love and make love with their eyes. Again, the irony is that I don't believe that blindness cripples a man sexually, and I think there exists no psychological evidence for it, but you don't read psychological textbooks to people when you are asking them to give their girl in marriage.

"Oh, you could get married in India all right, but not well, not happily, because the kind of girl you would want could not be found here. Once you have seen the other side of the coin, I mean a Western marriage, you will want a life companion equal to yourself.

"India is a harsh land. Marriage here is like a business transaction and people weigh and measure their liabilities and assets carefully. In the States, no doubt your blindness would make marriage difficult, though I believe not impossible, because there, values are different and marriage is made by the two people involved without the agency of parents. But all this you will find out only by living there.

"One more thing I would have you remember. In the melting pot of America, the problem of the Anglo-Indian does not exist, but here it does. At the same time your duty and service will never cease calling you back to India, where your roots lie deep."

The lonely image of my sister without her face was with me during the dinner and while Mr. DeFranco and I sat in the easy-chairs.

"There must be more," I stupidly insisted. Mr. DeFranco laughed and said, "There is really nothing more. Except," he added, "ours is one of those stories where they lived happily ever after."

Mrs. DeFranco came in from the kitchen and said to her husband, "Perhaps, dear, you could show him the apartment and the bath while I make his bed on the studio couch."

So Mr. DeFranco took me around his two-room apartment with the adjoining kitchen and bath, casually putting my hand over the screen separating the living-room from their bedroom, over the double bed, his writing-desk, the radio-phonograph combination in the living-room, and then the bathtub and the refrigerator. The apartment seemed to me small, in fact crowded, with barely enough space between the dining-room table and the radio-phonograph to allow one to pass through to the kitchen.

Mr. DeFranco said, however, "It is a very comfortable apartment for both of us and we are very happy in it."

My small studio-couch bed was made, and after formally saying good night to my hosts I climbed into it. I'm not going to think about anything, I thought; nothing, not even the empty, hollow feeling. You can at least think about the air hostess. Why can't you think about your mother? She didn't give you a lecture before you left home.

Mrs. DeFranco returned once more from behind the screen of their bedroom and quietly whispered, her breath warm, "I don't know whether you have refrigerators in India or not, but I didn't want you to worry at the noise of ours. The motor of our refrigerator makes dreadful sounds all through the night. I hope you don't mind."

"Not at all, Mrs. DeFranco," I said, turning my face up to her.

"Oh," she said, "I meant to tell you. Call me Muriel and my husband John."

"Of course," I barely said. "Good night, Muriel."

"Sweet dreams," she lightly said as she walked away behind the screen.

From *To Race the Wind*
Harold Krents

It was a misty evening in late October and a thick fog roamed the streets of Scarsdale. When I was a senior, we were a community of cliques. I have no idea how the outer circle of the "in" group or the inner circle of the "out" group spent this clammy Friday evening in late October, but I can report that the "in" group spent the time quite pleasantly, raising toast after toast to the great god Bacchus.

When we finally ran out of drinks, it was well past midnight.

"Last one in my Volkswagen has to drive," yelled Scott Brennan as he stumbled down the walk leading from Ted Turner's house.

Unfortunately, Scott forgot about the rather high step leading from the Turner's walk to the street below. Now over the years, I have fallen into many mud puddles. I consider myself to be an expert. I know that there is a real knack to falling into a mud puddle. Anybody can just plop into one, but it takes years of practice before one is able to land up to his ears in mud gracefully.

I have fallen many times but never with the artistry and skill which Scott Brennan exhibited that evening.

"Scott, you're drunk," cried out Brennan's girlfriend, Vicki Anderson, as she bumbled down the walk after her boyfriend.

A moment later the step claimed its second victim of the evening as Vicki joined Scott in the mud.

Sixty seconds later Dave Murdock, Corky Grant, and Sandy Sanders had continued the game of follow the leader. When I reached the fatal step, I stopped and squinted. Everything was flailing arms and legs and giggling, grunting, heaving mud-covered bodies. I spent the next five minutes attempting to load all five into Scott's Volkswagen sedan.

Six sober people in a stick-shift Volkswagen is at best unpleasant. If you multiply the discomfort by five thousand, you will only begin to approximate how miserable the ride which followed really was. Sandy Sanders was sitting on my lap, something which would have really thrilled me had the very lovely Miss Sanders been sober.

"You know, Hal," she burbled, "I liiikkeee yyyaa."

"I like you, too," I replied. The next moment I was locked in a tight embrace, being kissed by a one-hundred-and-three pound mud pie. As her lips met mine, I had the horrible sensation that I was kissing the Mojave Desert. When I tried to gasp for breath, my nostrils were filled with the scent of belched beer and bourbon. I think that I would have thrown up, had I not noticed something which made all of my other minor difficulties seem petty by comparison.

"Hey, Scott, you're not driving on the road anymore," I informed the driver.

"How da ya know?" he slurred.

"Because I don't hear the pleasant, comforting sound of concrete under those wheels."

The car came to a bumping halt, and Scott stumbled out to investigate.

"The blink is right." Scott hiccuped when he got back in the car. "I dunno where we are, but it's not on any road."

"I bet Hal could drive better than you," Sandy stammered drunkenly.

"Yeah, then let 'im try; I dar ya to try," retorted Scott.

"Things are bad enough without all of us getting killed," I said.

"Yah know something', Krents, you're a chickun, a goddamn blind chickun."

My entire social career was now squarely on the line.

"Okay, I'll drive," I chattered through trembling teeth. Scott slowly maneuvered his car back onto the street, and then a quick lesson ensued in which I was shown where the gas and the brake and the gearshift were located.

"Let 'er rip," roared Dave Murdock.

I turned the ignition, jammed the car into first gear, and pressed the gas pedal right down to the floor.

Suddenly, we were no longer in a 1957 Volkswagen; we were in a motorized earthquake.

"Clutch, clutch," Scott screamed as we continued to buck violently.

"I am, I am," I whimpered.

"I don't mean that kind of clutch. Press in the pedal up and to the right of the brake," my instructor roared back.

At long last I found the clutch and pressed it in, and to my amazement the car began to move slowly down the street.

"My driving career is under way at last," I crowed to those in the back seat.

It proved to be rather brief. Everything was proceeding just fine as we careened down the deserted woods-lined street until panic suddenly swept the back seat.

"We're going to die," moaned Corky, and I must confess that panic also rushed through the front seat.

I desperately wished that I, too, was squashed into that back seat, that is, until Sandy responded to this terrifying situation by throwing up on everything and everybody.

"Help, help," screamed Dave.

"Oh, go to hell," muttered Scott furiously.

"I'm already there," moaned Dave.

"When do I turn?" I asked, but I was totally ignored. Everybody was much too busy getting their souls in order preparatory to meeting their maker.

"Hey, when do I turn?" I yelled, but nobody bothered to throw a reply. It became clear that I was just going to have to operate on good old Krents's intuition. To this day, I think we would have made out just fine if only somebody had told me when to turn. As it was, however, my intuition must have taken the night off because I turned approximately twenty yards too soon. We careened off the road into the woods, and I calmly went for the brake. Unfortunately, in that moment of stress I had forgotten which pedal was the brake and which was the gas.

"Hey, Scott, where did you say the brake was?" I shrieked over my shoulder.

Fortunately for Scott and unfortunately for me, Scott had met this emergency in the manner he knew best—he passed out.

"On my own again," I muttered as we bumped through the undergrowth. "Well, things could be worse; there are only two pedals here, so I have a fifty percent chance of guessing right."

Once again I called upon my intuition and slammed down the pedal to my right just as hard as I could. Now the car was shooting through the undergrowth at a breakneck pace. Moments later by the process of elimination, I jammed on the brake, and the car came to a screeching halt in the rhododendron bush of somebody's front lawn.

"Am I dead? Is this paradise?" moaned Dave Murdock after a long moment of silence.

"Well, what do we do now?" asked Corky.

"Don't ask me, I'm just the chauffeur." I laughed.

"Listen, cut out the jokes and come up with something constructive. As things stand right now, I'm in trouble up to my ass," snapped Dave.

"I've got it," said Vicki brightly. "When the police arrive, we'll tell them that Scott was driving me, Sandy, Corky, and Dave home from a party when we picked up a blind hitchhiker. No sooner had we begun to drive than this hitchhiker knocked Scott out and hijacked the car with all of us in it."

"I don't think it'll work, Vick," said Dave. "But please keep thinking. As a matter of fact, you'd better think real fast because here comes a police car right now." He gasped.

"Hey, he's using my new highway," I exclaimed angrily.

"Well, demand that he pay you a toll when he gets here," suggested Corky.

"Okay, kid, hand over your license," said a young-sounding policeman the moment he reached our car.

"I don't have a license, sir," I gulped.

"Just as I suspected." The policeman grunted. "You don't look eighteen."

"Oh, I'm eighteen all right, but I just don't happen to own a license," I responded.

"You know, of course, that we could really throw the book at you," he continued.

"I know that, but I'd never catch it—I'm blind, totally blind."

"You're drunk," he snapped.

"Perhaps a bit of that, too, but also blind. Hey, have you ever heard the expression blind drunk, well, now you're seeing one in real life."

"Get out here and walk in a straight line," he snarled.

"Gosh, I wish I could, but really it's quite impossible. You see I can't ever walk a straight line—drunk or sober."

I could tell from his labored breathing that his composure was beginning to fade. He immediately commenced to snap his fingers in front of my face. Now I have been informed that sighted people flinch when this is done. As he quickly discovered, blind people do not.

"Is he really blind? I mean *blind* blind?" the officer asked Dave.

"Like a bat," Dave replied cheerily.

"That doesn't help at all," he mumbled. "The problem is simply how I'm going to go back to the police station and report the discovery of a car in the middle of a guy's rhododendron bush driven by a blind man. They'll never believe it.

"Listen, I'm going to forget about this entire nightmare on the condition that you solemnly swear never to drive again."

"I'm perfectly willing to swear to that."

With Heironymous Bosch in India
Irving Kenneth Zola

I had expected many unusual things of India but the welcoming remarks were not among them. As I walked from my plane, a government official, a Sikh, resplendent in his turban, rushed forward through the crowd to greet me. After we introduced ourselves and shook hands, he asked in quick succession, "Where in the States are you from? From where was your undergraduate degree? Your graduate degree? And what happened to your leg?"

The latter, as any American would know, was hardly a typical opening between strangers. I answered in turn, "Boston, Harvard A.B., Harvard Ph.D.," and then, somewhat hesitatingly, "polio complicated by an auto accident." The question bothered me and I began to wonder about Sikhs.

When we reached our car, I was introduced to his colleague, a Tamil, who asked about my home, my schooling and what happened to my leg. The next several hours produced more of the same. Whether it was heads of bureaus or governmental ministers, the introductory questions varied little. My responses on the other hand seemed to be taken as but pertinent bits of information to be received and stored. I was curious, even a little put out at this intrusion into what Americans regard as so private a matter. It had been many years since I was made directly aware that I wore a back support and a long leg brace, used a cane, and walked with a limp. But I decided to ignore it and turn my attention to the business at hand. This was, however, an omen of things to come, of an event a week hence which would make me acutely conscious of "what happened to my leg."

On Friday afternoon at about 2:00 p.m., I was outside the posh Oberoi Hotel. It was hot and dry, nearly 100 degrees in the shade, but my excitement overcame my usual dislike of heat. A week of conferences had been interesting but today was to be my first "adventure." After touring several impressive medical facilities, I was anxious to see something more local, and secretly, I thought, more real. In response to my request, colleagues had arranged a visit with an Ayurvedic healer, a local folk physician. And so I waited and wondered about the questions I would ask.

A horn sounded and the bus, marked with the familiar World Health Organization symbol, pulled up. In the rear seats I could see my guides for the day, Doctors T. and M. They waved and I saluted back. Paying more attention to Dr. M., who looked exquisite again in a sari, I pushed myself to a standing position. As I did, I heard a crack. It sounded as if it came from within me, but I felt all together. As I stepped toward the bus, there was an unpleasant squeaking and clicking sound. I climbed in and when I sat, my trouble became obvious. Something was trying to poke its way through the knee of my trousers. The brace, one I had had for 15 years, had snapped somewhere just below the knee.

Here I was, thousands of miles from home, in a strange land, without friends and, needless to say, without a spare brace, on my way (of all things) to see an Ayurvedic healer. I had certain confidence in his ability to deal with a myriad of problems, but a welder he was not!

I turned, hesitatingly, to my hosts. "Ah," I stammered eloquently, "I seem to have a problem," and pointed to my leg. Unfortunately, as an explanation, this did not suffice, so with great embarrassment, I rolled up my trousers to show the dangling part.

"No problem," they said and gave the driver new directions.

By this time I was soaking in sweat—partly through anxiety and partly because this enclosed bus felt like an oven.

Within a few minutes we arrived at a series of low-lying buildings, paint peeling and baked a dull orange by the sun. With an air of confidence that I lacked, Dr. T. identified the place as the Nehru Rehabilitation Center. As I limped toward the door a hundred yards away, the "clickety-clack" of my brace seemed to announce my coming. Neither the appearance of the building nor my first glimpse of its occupants reassured me.

I was confronted by what I can only describe as a Hieronymous Bosch painting in all-*too*-living color. While my Indian colleagues explained to those in charge about my trouble, I was trying to absorb—or rather deny—the scene before my eyes. Within uncomfortable touching distance was a panoramic history of physical suffering. An old man in a turban, toothless, blind in one eye, with his right foot missing below the ankle, stood quite straight, leaning on a makeshift crutch; a young man, twentyish, wandered around, speaking to many but with no one returning the attention; countless children limped to and fro; still younger ones, some with shriveled limbs, some crying, some just staring, were held and occasionally rocked by their mothers. So many people had missing extremities that I flashed to "read-about" scenes of wartime surgeries, where, one after another, limbs are amputated, cast aside, and stacked in piles. Hardest to take were those who moved about in what felt like grotesque ways. Kneeling on a cart, a man in his mid-twenties pushed himself forward with his hands—a Porgy without his grandeur. Another with no legs used his hands to hop from place to place with a slowness that was painful.

But this was no whining mass of humanity as in the Bosch pictures. If anything, there was an air of resignation. And I seemed to be the only one showing signs of discomfort. As my stomach did flip-flops, I wondered what the hell I was doing here. Why did I leave safe Geneva for this? After days of hearing of the problems in the delivery of medical services, was I about to experience it first-hand? This was far beyond the limits of my intended participant-observation.

The appearance of an eight-year-old boy helped curb my anxiety. He was wearing a long leg brace just like mine. I wanted to shout for joy. It meant they could really help me. Guiltily, I realized it also meant that at least some of the younger generation were receiving up-to-date rehabilitative care.

I heard Dr. M. call me and then saw Dr. T. approaching. "Everything will be taken care of and we will pick you up in about two hours. All right?"

I nodded my head in agreement, not really meaning it. Were they really going to leave me here? Alone? I was bothered by my own thoughts. What was it I feared? And so acting braver than I felt, I shrugged my shoulders. Directed to a bench, I limped over and sat down. From this less vertical position I felt even more overwhelmed, almost suffocated, but I didn't know why. After all the time I'd spent in hospitals, I was surprised at my reaction. But just as suddenly I understood. My hospital time was spent amongst people who were getting better or struggling to. Troubles here were chronic and the patients not likely to improve.

Maybe my thoughts showed, for soon people began to introduce themselves and explain the surroundings. They were trying to be helpful and friendly but I could not understand a word. So I only smiled in return. Then as if he had hit on the source of my discomfort, a young man said something to the man beside him. When his bearded seatmate nodded approval, the young man excitedly jumped up, and dragging his left foot, rushed off through the crowd. In a few minutes he returned. In his outstretched hand was an opened bottle of Coke.

My stomach sank and I hesitated. I remembered that just two days earlier my WHO colleagues and I had been wedded to our toilets because of dysentery contracted from drinking water. Was I going to go through all this again?

Noting my despair, he smiled knowingly and took the first drink himself. Turning to the crowd who had gathered around us, he nodded his head and handed me the bottle. Embarrassed, and I suppose grateful for this kindness, I couldn't resist. I drank and then passed the bottle. Everyone seemed pleased, including me.

There was little time to relish my bravery before a clerk in a long white coat appeared, "Dr. Zola, please come with me and we will take care of you." Out of the corner of my eye I noticed someone carrying a young boy out of a cubicle. It was to that place that I was directed.

"You'll be more comfortable here. So please take off your brace."

He left and I looked around. He had closed the tattered curtain, which provided, at best, only a psychological sense of privacy. The table on which I was supposed to sit held a pool of urine—perhaps left by the young child made anxious when he was carried out so quickly to make room for me. I was upset but it made little sense to insist that he be brought back to his puddle. So I sat on the rickety chair, took off my trousers, removed my brace, dressed again and then limped out, now moving more slowly and unsteadily, brace in hand, its right side cracked and dangling. I handed it this time to a young woman in white.

Calmer now, I returned to my bench. All I could do was watch the hubbub. People were going back and forth, but because of their often lurching movements it all appeared like a movie in slow motion.

A wheelchair came bounding through the door and a young teenage boy with dark curly hair, muscular above the waist, withered below, gave a piece of paper to the clerk. Then I noticed that many of them had pieces of paper in their hands. But I had nothing. Nothing to do. Nothing to read. No one to talk to. More confused than scared, I smiled at the children, and they smiled back. Amidst the rags and disfigurements, one thing began to stand out—all the medical staff in their stiff, white, gleaming coats. All these men and women looked so young, so beautiful, so handsome. Was it just that they were healthy and we were not? Or were they chosen, maybe motivated to work in such a place because of their appearance? I kept thinking of all the times I had sat at the mercy of a dentist, while his dental hygienist, with sparkling, cavity-free teeth, proceeded to pick at my gums and instruct me about the perils of failing to brush properly.

My reverie was eventually interrupted. "Dr. Zola, it's ready." I rose and there was my brace—repaired and straight. Once again I was directed to the cubicle and I began to dress.

A head poked in. "I wonder if you would mind coming out or just standing there with your brace." For a moment I did not grasp the man's meaning. He continued, "It would be nice for them. So that they could see their work."

More out of gratitude than understanding, I rose and walked forward through the entrance. My trousers were draped over my arm and there I stood— above the waist, a jacket, shirt, and tie, and below, undershorts, with my brace and me more exposed than usual. With barely a glance, the attendant announced my presence and called for the staff to appear.

Still another shock awaited me. There were five men: one missing an arm and a leg, one on crutches, one with a withered arm, and off to the side a husky man, who carried in his arms a co-worker whose legs dangled as helplessly and lifelessly as my brace had a few hours before. Part of the hubbub was now clear to me, the people with pieces of paper going back and forth had been carrying messages and order forms. For the past several hours I had been not only at a rehabilitation center, but a sheltered workshop.

I thanked everyone, proudly pointed to my brace and even shook my leg as if to indicate its regained strength. They smiled, giggled, and left. I finished dressing and looked around. And there to one side were my WHO colleagues. I was glad to see them and glad to leave. I was sure that I was fleeing something but I didn't know what. Perhaps guilty that I could leave and that, in a sense, these people could not? Guilty even that I felt quite restored to normal society, even whole again. Without knowing my thoughts, my companions reaffirmed this with an Americanism,

"You look as good as new." I was uncomfortably elated with this cliche. As we walked to the car, they asked, almost perfunctorily, about the care I had received. When I said "Fine," they asked no more and went on to talk about the next stop on our itinerary.

Like the opening words of greeting a week ago, my three-hour experience was just another piece of information, just another incident in their busy day, recorded and quickly forgotten. But not for me, not for me.

From *First You Cry*
by Betty Rollin

The phony tit wasn't making it. I couldn't get the goddam thing to stay down. Even when I fastened it with a safety pin and lowered the left bra strap to zero, after a half hour or so the entire amalgamation rose like a buoy. It stayed down more when I hooked the bra tighter around me, but then it dug into the part of the wound that dipped under my arm, and that hurt. Also, the damn thing had no nipple. That wouldn't have mattered if my own remaining nipple didn't show, but God or whoever hands out nipples gave me a perpetually erect one. The only solution was a return trip to the tit shop to buy a proper made-to-order one-half-pound breast.

The second visit was, to be sure, less jarring than the first. But to my surprise and disappointment they did not sell—nor, they said, did anyone else sell—made-to-order prosthetic breasts. (That turned out not to be true.) They did have breasts in graduated sizes, however (like shoes!), and they were sure they could fix me up. The sales pitch amused me. Tits for sale: a business like any other. I wondered if it went the same way in the leg-and-arm biz.

They did, indeed, have a prosthesis in my size. It was silicone and it was soft and pink and weighty. But it didn't have a nipple. Uh, I said, do you have one with a nipple? A nipple? they said. What an idea! They had no nipples, except for flat ones that were sort of drawn onto the form; nothing that stuck out. In a low voice I explained the problem of my idiosyncratically erect right nipple. The silence could not have been stonier had I announced syphilis. I picked up my Dacron wad, shoved it into my bra (without pinning it, so that by the time I got home it had edged up into the vicinity of my collarbone), and got out of there.

Swell, I thought. Wonderful. I was an outcast in the land of outcasts. I was not only a one-titted woman in a two-titted world, I was an erect-nippled one-titted woman in a flat-nippled one-titted world. I thought of a musical piece for children I had seen on television a few weeks earlier—Harry Nilsson's *The Point*—about a little boy with a round head who lives in a place where everyone has a pointed head, so they banish him to a forest where it doesn't matter if your head is round because no one else is there.

I called Reach to Recovery. Yes, they knew of a made-to-order place. In California. I called the man in California. Yes, he did make nipples. Yes, his "forms," as he called them, did have to be worn inside a bra, and yes, he would send me a brochure.

The problem was I had begun to do on-camera work again during the day; we were going out more at night. I felt that I could not go one more day without a nipple. Whereupon it occurred to me that perhaps I could make one myself—attach something small and pointed to the nylon cover of the Dacron wad. I headed for my sewing box, rummaged through spools of thread, buttons, pincushions, and cards of needles and pins, and there, in one corner of the box, under a green button, was a black nipple. Actually, it was a black cloth cuff link. But I knew right away it would work. I pulled up my blouse and held it next to my right nipple. Perfect.

That is, the size and shape were perfect. The color, black, was not perfect. But what the hell. I wasn't planning to wear any see-through blouses.

Just as I threaded a needle and went to work, Arthur came home. "What are you doing?" he said.

"I just invented a nipple and I'm sewing it on," I said. "Now I know how Eli Whitney felt."

The next aim was to make it work without a bra. A few days later, I bought a roll of surgical body tape and, with two strips on top and two on the bottom, taped my newly nippled prosthesis onto my body. Then I pulled on a T-shirt and looked at myself, first front, then side. It was magnificent. Really magnificent. I couldn't wait to show those harpies at the tit store—if I ever went back there again, which I probably would have to, to get a bathing suit. Meanwhile, it took a good deal of restraint not to pull my top up and show everyone I knew what I had wrought.

But I did restrain myself. The pride of invention was strong, but not as strong as the other feeling: the continual, reigning, omnipresent sense of being deformed. It turned me into something I had never been before: a modest woman. There is a boutique I used to like on Fifty-third Street. I walked in there one day—not very long ago—and walked straight out. I had forgotten about the group dressing room.

To hide in public seemed to me sensible and considerate. To hide at home was, I knew, something else. So far, only three people had seen me without a bandage: Dr. Singermann, Dr. Singermann's nurse, and myself. Sooner or later, Arthur would have to see me too. I couldn't keep hiding in my own house. I had sort of wished he had asked to see me, but he didn't. So one evening, while I was sitting in the bathtub, I asked him. "Arthur," I yelled.

"What?" he yelled back, from the other side of the bathroom door.

"C'mere," I said.

He opened the door slowly. The unwritten rule, since bandage removal, was that my baths were private. He peeked in. My left hand and arm were covering my left side.

"Wanna see?" I asked.

"Sure," he said, looking uncomfortable.

Suddenly, it didn't seem like such a good idea. But it was too late. "Look," I said, and, keeping my eyes on his face, slowly I lowered my left arm.

He didn't flinch. "That's not so bad," he said. I shrugged. "It doesn't bother me a bit," he added, protesting a little too much.

"That's good," I said, slipping back under the water.

At a glance, the prosthesis brochure from California looked like something from a computer dating operation. MATCH-MATE, said the letters in big black type on a blue background, and, in smaller letters, Breast Prosthesis. Inside there was a drawing of a woman (wearing what I think was meant to look like a sexy dress) about to serve dinner to a man who was hovering over her adoringly. Restore Poise and Self-Confidence, dot, dot, dot, it said. And, on the other pages there were twenty Questions and Answers, e.g.: Q. Is the MATCH-MATE prosthesis filled with liquid? A. Definitely not! Accidental piercing of this type could be extremely embarrassing. Nor is MATCH-MATE the foam rubber type which can absorb perspiration and deteriorate. Farther down, it said that MATCH-MATE was made of a "special vinyl plastic" which is "chemically inert, which means it is not affected by body perspiration or other outside elements." (Like what, I wondered. Sleet and snow? Fire and water?)

It looked OK, but California was still a long way to go for a couple of ounces of vinyl. I decided to pay a call on Terese Lasser (the Reach to Recovery head) over at the American Cancer Society. Mrs. Lasser was reputed to know everything there is to know about prosthetic devices. On the phone, she had been first to confirm this. "If I don't know about it," she had said, "it doesn't exist."

Mrs. Lasser is an ample woman in her middle fifties and has what used to be called an imposing air. When I walked into her office, she was seated behind a big desk piled high with photographs, letters, and rubber breasts. The photographs and letters, which she showed me immediately, were of and from women who had had mastectomies. She held up one of the photographs—of a bride. "Isn't it wonderful?" she said. I agreed that it was wonderful and moved right on to the tale of my search for the perfect breast.

Before I got to the part about the nipple, she got up and went over to a cabinet on the other side of the room. "Try this," she said brightly, tossing me a pink blob that looked similar to the blobs from the tit store. No nipple. But it did have some weight. I looked at it more closely and gave it a squeeze. "It feels nice," I said, "but I think it's too big."

"I don't have a smaller one," said Mrs. Lasser. "Try it." I put it in my left bra cup. "Perfect," she said. It wasn't.

"Don't you think it's a little too big?" I asked meekly.

She sprang up again and pulled open another drawer. She came toward me with some Dacron stuffing. "Try putting this in the other one." Obediently, I stuffed the Dacron in my right bra cup. "There, that's fine," said Mrs. Lasser, with a case-closed clap of her hands. (There were two other women waiting outside and someone else on the phone.) I gave myself a quick once-over in the full-length mirror on the back of her door. I was now bigger-breasted than I had ever been in my whole life. I thanked Mrs. Lasser—who, I felt, had done her best—put my own prosthesis in my purse, rounded my shoulders, and sped home, hoping I could get there without running into anyone I knew.

The next day I decided to try to improve the cuff-link-cum-nipple concept. Happily, there was a branch of the Singer Sewing Machine Company right in Rockefeller Center, very near NBC. After work I went over and headed straight for the button department. "Do you have any cloth buttons?" I asked a portly saleswoman with a permanent wave. No, she said, but here were the buttons they did have. There were hundreds, separated by color. I edged over to the tans and browns. This looks good, I said to myself, picking up a card of round, light brown buttons that looked soft. I felt one. It was plastic and not soft at all. There were some lighter brown ones nearby. They were also too hard and too big. The lady with the permanent wave was looking at me as if I were doing something dirty with her buttons. I moved away and found myself in front of the fringe counter. Wrapped around foot-high pieces of cardboard, there was enough fringe to hang the White House.

I stopped. On the bottom row, there were cards of ball fringe. Balls. One of the fringes was a sort of golden brown. I zeroed in on the balls. They were the size of nipples and the color of nipples—well, maybe Oriental ones. Good enough, I thought, trying not to look too excited. I bent over and gave one of the balls a little feel. Soft as a cooked pea. I looked behind me. Permanent Wave was still staring. I straightened up. "I'll take that," I said with a show of authority.

She pulled out the card. "How much do you want?" she said, taking it over to the table yardstick.

I thought, I can't ask for one ball: "One quarter of a yard," I said.

She gave me a look. "The minimum we sell is a half yard."

"That'll be fine," I said. She rang up the sale; I handed her twenty-six cents and fled.

As soon a I got home, I pulled my sweater up for the old comparison test. Very good. Very, very good. I snipped off the cuff link with a nail scissors and sewed on the new nipple. It was gorgeous, absolutely gorgeous. There were seven more balls on the rest of the half yard that was left. Seven spares. I put them in my sewing box. Eight nipples for a quarter, I thought, feeling better than I had in days. Not bad.

When I went to take the prosthesis back to Mrs. Lasser, I noticed another woman outside her office, reading a magazine. She was about my age and pretty in a quiet, sweet way. Then my eyes dropped to her chest. She was wearing a T-shirt, and the difference in her breasts was so obvious I gasped. One breast was round and the other one was absurdly pointed. Unlike mine, her pointed one looked like the phony, not the round one. That was because the point didn't look like a nipple. It looked like the bottom of a paper drinking cup. Well, I thought, Mrs. Lasser will straighten her out.

Mrs. Lasser, meanwhile, motioned for me to come in and close the door. "*That* poor girl," she said, in a stage whisper. "She's only three weeks out of the hospital and her husband expects her to do *everything*." (She lingered meaningfully on the "everything.") "He's pushing her much too hard." I asked her what she meant. "He thinks the way to handle things is to push and she is very upset by it. I had a talk with him, but I don't know if it'll do any good." I said I was sure one of her little talks couldn't help but have an effect.

"How, by the way, are most husbands in this situation?" I asked her.

"Great," she said. "Mostly, it's the woman herself who is not so great."

The worst problem between husbands and wives, Mrs. Lasser went on to say, was misunderstanding. Sometimes the husband would try to be considerate and not press the wife about sex, for example, and the wife would interpret this as a loss of desire on his part. Or, she said, sometimes the husband would press too much. "But the biggest problem is not how their husbands feel about them, but how the women feel about themselves."

She stopped and looked at me. Then, seeing how interested I was, she went on. She knew women who couldn't bear to look at themselves—ever. She knew one woman who killed herself, another who slept in a separate bed from her husband the rest of her life. I asked her if a woman's age figured in her reaction to the operation. "Age has *nothing* to do with it, she said emphatically. "It has much more to do with vanity." The woman who killed herself was in her sixties. But she was an ex-opera singer and, in spite of her age, she thought of herself as being beautiful. When this thing happened to her, she simply couldn't take it. Of course, with extreme cases like that, there were always other problems as well.

"I better go now," I heard myself say to Mrs. Lasser. "Thanks for everything." Suddenly, I couldn't wait to get out. Although I found them engrossing, those stories did not have the same effect they had had on me when I was in the hospital. Other women's grief, now that I had experienced some myself, no longer cheered me up. On the contrary—although it was no fault of hers—Mrs. Lasser's tales depressed me the rest of that day and then some. I couldn't get the paper-cup woman's face out of my head. It's still there.

I took a bus uptown and another picture flashed into my head, the one of Betty Ford, waving on the balcony of the White House. I thought again of how much publicity there had been about those famous women and their bravery, and I realized more than ever how little publicity there was—none, really—about their dark days. Naturally (but why naturally?) if they had dark days they would have to hide them.

It was all very inspiring, those famous chins-up—but I wonder how many women might have been helped even more if they heard about the sad stuff as well. If ever I write about this, I vowed on the Third Avenue bus that day, I will tell about my sad stuff and let the other sufferers know they have company. And let the brave women feel braver still by comparison.

But for now I was on leave from the sadness and darkness. The prosthesis problem was, of course, a splendid distraction. Looking back, I'm sure that's largely why it became such an obsession. No doubt about it; the best way to stop worrying about something is not to try *not* to worry, or to focus on "something pleasant," but to work up a whole new worry about something *else*. The beauty of the breast hunt was that, unlike weaving baskets or pounding clay, it was not obviously therapeutic. At least not to me. As far as I was concerned, it was normal to spend most of one's waking hours thinking about breasts and detachable nipples.

Not that I was able to insulate myself completely from dark thoughts and feelings. Sometimes they just snuck up from behind, like the reaction I had to Mrs. Lasser's stories. Other bad moments came like smacks in the back of the head. One day, for example, after my arm had more or less returned to working order, I decided to resume my calisthenics, which I used to do every day for five minutes and end by running in place one hundred times. I did not wear a bra when I exercised, so when I got to the running part I would always hold onto my breasts to keep them from bouncing. That day, after sit-ups and bicycle kicks, I began the final run-in-place and both hands went up, as they had always done, to hold my breasts. But in a couple of seconds my brain sent a reminder to my left hand that there was nothing for it to hold. I dropped my hand and kept on running, but I had to stop before reaching one hundred because I was crying too hard.

Months later, on a short holiday, at a pool in Key Biscayne, Florida, I was wearing my new prosthesis inside a specially sewn-in pocket in my bathing suit top (which was also stiched up an extra inch in the middle to hide the still puffy pink scar), so I no longer had the "prosthesis problem" to distract me. Time had gone by and it was a beautiful day and I lay on the deck chair with the sun high and hot overhead and my mind was far from the place on my chest where a breast had been. Then I looked up and saw a girl walk by in an extremely brief fuchsia bikini who began to strut, sort of, around the edge of the pool. She had very large breasts. I started to read, but every time I looked up I

could see her sashaying back and forth toward the div-
ing board and back and forth again. I tried to keep on
reading, but she kept strutting and I kept looking up,
and before I realized what had happened to me I was
sobbing horribly. I had sunglasses, luckily, to hide my
eyes, but no tissues, so I stumbled inside and ran up to
the hotel room. It took about an hour before I was
ready to leave the room, and I never did make it back
to the pool.

That incident was no worse than several similar stabs
of breast envy that had happened early on. But it hit
me harder because it occurred when I no longer expected to feel that way. As I began to feel less awful
about what had happened, I think I unconsciously expected it to "end"—the way my friend Joanna's broken
hip had ended, the way most bad things I knew about
ended. These incidents reminded me that, although I
felt better about what had happened and would, no
doubt, grow to feel still better, "what had happened"
would never really end. Not ever.

After two weeks of research, I finally went to Ann
Arbor, Michigan, where, in the basement of the
University's Medical Center, I was greeted by Denis
Lee, a made-to-order prosthesis maker who swore he
could make me a nipple that stuck out. From his name,
I had expected him to be Chinese, but he wasn't. He
was a sturdy young midwestern American whose
father is a dentist. Mr. Lee's father's profession, it turned out, had no small bearing on his son's trade.

Mr. Lee's technique of prosthesis-making involves
taking the same kind of impression that dentists take,
only you are the tooth. That is, you sit in a chair (which
looks very much like a dentist's chair) and with a bib

around your waist, instead of around your neck, an impression is made of your chest, almost exactly the same way as an impression is made of your tooth. It sounded altogether logical when Mr. Lee explained it to me, but I admit that when I was actually seated in the chair, stripped to the waist, and he approached me with a yellow mixing bowl full of a substance that looked like overcooked oatmeal and proceeded to smear it all over my upper body with a plastic spatula, I had my doubts.

The "oatmeal," he had told me earlier, was an alginate which hardens into a rubber consistency the same way it does in the mouth. Needless to say, when it is your chest it doesn't *feel* the same. (At first, it feels repulsive and cold and then, after ten minutes, it feel repulsive and warm.)

Before the substance hardened, Mr. Lee came toward me with another mixing bowl filled with what looked like creamier oatmeal. This was plaster. He then smeared the creamy oatmeal over the lump oatmeal and topped it off by wrapping me up in gauze so that, he explained, the substance would keep its shape.

When the mess had hardened and I was beginning to wonder how he was planning to get me out of what was now a firm cast, Mr. Lee picked at the top with his fingers, gave it a little pull, and the whole thing peeled off as if it were a banana skin.

"This, you see, is a negative," he said, taking my rubberized configuration into the next room. "Now we fill it with plaster," he shouted so that I could hear him, "and we get a positive, and then we sculpt a replica of the one breast in clay and then we take another cast of that, and *then*," he said, coming back into the room where I was still sitting half naked with the hardened porridge all over my plastic apron, "we make the prosthesis by painting a special mixture of silicone and a catalyst onto the new cast and when it gets hard, we peel it off, fill it up with glycerine, using a little more or a little less glycerine to get the right weight, and we put a backing on it, and that's it!"

"That's really interesting," I said, struggling to get out of the chair.

"Let me help you," he said, and hoisted me down. "Oh—before you get dressed, let's have a look at these." He went over to a cabinet next to the wall and pulled out a few cards of paint samples, mostly tan and some brown.

"What are they for?" I asked.

"That's so we get the right color." He held up one card to the skin of my right breast. "That looks pretty good. . . . It's funny, most women, no matter what the rest of their skin tone is, usually have breasts of this one color." I said yes, that was funny, and wondered what he was doing with the other samples. "Now we match the nipple color," he said, holding up the darker tans next to my nipple. "Hmmm, maybe if we use this and add just a touch of blue." He snapped together the cards. "OK, you can get dressed now."

He went back into the other room while I put my bra and prosthesis and blouse on. When I joined him, he was sitting behind a desk, and I didn't see what was on the desk until he said, "I thought you might like to see what else we do," and then I looked down and there on his green blotter were three ears, two fingers, and a nose.

"Aren't they nice" I said, without moving nearer. "Who are those for?"

"People who have lost other parts of their bodies because of cancer or injuries. I had a woman come in this morning; she was fooling around with one of those power mowers and—*whap!*—there went her third finger."

"Are one of those her—new finger?" I said, trying not to point.

"Oh, no, hers won't be ready for a couple of weeks...I won't have yours until then, either."

I wanted to ask Mr. Lee some more questions, preferably without the digit and features display between us. On the other hand, I didn't want to hurt his feelings by asking him to take them away. I decided to proceed and try to keep my eyes on his face. "How come," I asked him, "made-to-order prostheses are so hard to get? I should think every woman who has had a breast removed would want as exact a replica as she can get."

He shrugged. "Women want them, all right. But they're hard to make. A lot of people have tried and it hasn't worked out. The backs have been irritating or they were too heavy. A million things can go wrong." He smiled. "Terese Lasser has a theory about why there are so few good prostheses. Want to know what it is?"

"Sure," I said.

"She says it's because mastectomies only happen to women. She says if they cut men's testicles off, they would have worked up a great replacement by now."

I laughed. "She's probably right," I said, and then, having forgotten about the display, my eyes moved down to the desk blotter. I looked up at once. "Well, I better get going," I said.

"I'll walk you out to where you can get a taxi," said Mr. Lee, who was really very sweet.

We walked down a long corridor and up to the main floor and out the door. I got into a taxi. "Thanks *very* much," I said. "Good-bye."

"Good-bye," he said, with a nice grin, bending down so that he could see me through the car window. "There's just one thing," he said. "We have had a couple of problems with these things. Uh—if it leaks, just let me know." And the car sped away.

From *Episode*
Eric Hodgins

It was with true eagerness that I awaited the arrival of Miss Wimple, who was to be my permanent night nurse. The evening she first appeared seemed deeply propitious. She rang in at 7:45 p.m. for an 8-to-8 night. Her looks were lovely. She was blonde, tall, stately but shapely, with exquisite Continental manners, murmurously deferential to Miss Hants and to me. I felt a distinct uptrend in my low spirits when a carnal thought, for the first time in months, crossed my mind. Miss Wimple spoke perfect English, delightfully tinged with a foreignness which was almost, but not quite, British. After Miss Hants left, Miss Wimple and I settled down for a cosy evening, I lolling back in my chair, she sitting earnestly on its footstool and, in the European tradition, presenting to me personally her letters of recommendation endorsed by a wide variety of Herr-Doktor-Professors from spas and health resorts the like of which the United States does not possess. Even when written in languages I could not understand, they were impressive.

Things were off to a flying start. At 10 p.m. Miss Wimple offered me my sleeping capsules, and I actually liked her use of the Infant Plural: "Shall we take our little pills now?" She ushered me to my bed, handsomely turned down, and with a lovely decorum, withdrew. I was sorry to see her go. But whatever vague and formless notions may have been gathering in my drowsy, pill-riddled mind, they were due to blow up nine hours and fifteen minutes later. On the dot.

I slept well that night. At 7:15 the next morning Miss Wimple, a vision in white (she looked as well by day as by night), entered with a tray upon which there stood a glass of orange juice of just the size I have always really wanted. Had I slept well? I had. Had she? Splendidly. I seemed far from any possible abyss.

I arose and brushed my teeth. Resuming my bed, I picked up the glass of orange juice, took my first grateful sip and put the glass down with an unsettling crash. The orange juice was hot. I do not mean it was carelessly warm; I mean it had been deliberately heated. Like a leper, I rang the leper's bell at my bedside. Miss Wimple's graceful form appeared, her sweet young woman's face set in a look of gentle inquiry. Without words (because there were no words) I indicated that I was not partial to hot or even warm orange juice. A hot Scotch-and-soda, administered in cardiac cases, I had heard of, but never experienced. I could, however, contemplate it. I could not contemplate hot orange juice. I got my bang out of the morning's orange juice because it was icy cold, Miss Wimple, please, in the name of. . . .

"But that is not *gude* for you," said Miss Wimple.

. . . My mind had begun going strange places, unbidden. Where it went now, as I pondered how to counter Miss Wimple, was *The Conning Tower* as conducted by Franklin P. Adams in those lovely days, the teens and twenties of this now old and unlovely century.

One of F.P.A.'s contribs ("Chicot") had been blessed by the idea of *Journalistic Jingles*, in which he systematically went through every cliche of every department of the daily press. Not unnaturally, this morning, my memory called up two of his entries for *The Obit Column:*

I

Timothy Fitzgerald, a printer on the *Herald*,
Died in bed on Sunday at the age of fifty-three.
　　No human soul was finer,
　　He was a Mystic Shriner.
He leaves a wife, Maria, and a daughter, Marjorie.

II

Professor P.T. Holley, run down by a trolley,
Tuesday last, succumbed this morning to a
fractured spine.
　　An expert dietetic,
　　His end was almost pathetic,
Burial at Woodlawn, Monday morning, sharp
at nine.

I did not know which of those two lucky ones I wished the more to be. I did not even know whether my death wish was directed against myself or against the dietetics (not of Prof. Holley) to which I was now being subjected. Through the mists of these confusions I could hear Miss Wimple saying, "We must help Nature build up the *boddy* to combat the shock it has sustained." This sounded irreproachable, but if it implied hot orange juice I was not sure the *boddy*, mine anyhow, instinctively wished what was best for it. And at this stage of affairs, I did not know the half of it.

Slowly as the days went on it dawned on me, the custody into which I had fallen. It was the custody of Good Women. Miss Hants and Miss Wimple made a sort of crosshatched pattern. Miss Hants, the elder, was gray, authoritarian and Good. Miss Wimple, the younger, was eager, full of earnest persuasiveness and Good. Of the two, I think Miss Wimple was the Gooder. In life's hard school I lived to learn that Good Women, although united in spirituality, do not necessarily like one another. The few moments of every day when Miss Hants and Miss Wimple met, morn and eve, began to crackle with acrimony. Their views on Method were different. They had no vices but even their non-vices were non-similar. Each had a tendency to use her Goodness to protect me from the undesirable Goodness of the other. Things finally became clearer to me when I realized I was the object of a contest: each Good Woman wanted to shoot a goal with me; through them I learned what it felt like to be a hockey puck.

Miss Hants was bosom-deep in Inspiration; a religionist of some Theosophist-Steineresque-plus-whatever-was-on-Sunday-morning-TV kind, whose sincerity I could not for an instant question but whose substance, as God is my witness, I could not appraise. Daily, daily, and twice on Sundays, she uncorked some new Positive Thought on me, and I grew numb under these successive assaults. For night duty Miss Wimple's Spirituality expressed itself differently: she never directly alluded to the Deity, to Christianity or to any of its Apostles, ancient or modern. It took me some time to get a Heavenly fix on her, but when I did I labeled her a Chlorophyll-Carotene-Pantheist, for she truly and honestly believed that enough carrot juice, particularly if laced with alfalfa, would cure any disease going, including cancer. "It is true; I am not joking; I have seen it." The varieties of religious experience I was encountering now had never, I felt sure, been revealed to William James. I wish they had been. He would have known what to do. I did not.

One evening Miss Wimple astounded me by asking, in her prettiest way—and her ways were very pretty—might she have a cigarette? Since my own cigarette habit had been a source of constant, gentle sorrow for her, I had a wild moment of imagining I had achieved a corruption, but the thought died at birth when she explained that she permitted herself four cigarettes a year, and a time had come. With a shaking hand I gave her not only the cigarette but a light. She made the cigarette last about a half hour, vigorously expelling its combustion products (carbon monoxide, contaminated water vapor and carcinogenic tars) before they should touch her uvula. Then our debauch was over. Unfortunately I had been used to madder music and stronger wine; I wound up the evening feeling even more immorally inferior than ever to Baudelaire, Rimbaud and Verlaine. The consolations of the most ordinary kinds of booze, to say nothing of absinthe or mescal, were denied me by a variety of circumstances. I knew less than a modern high-school girl about how to come into illegal possession of narcotics. And I was on a low-cholesterol, low-sodium diet—something to cancel every page of joy in Mrs. Rombauer's cookbook.

Nevertheless, in Miss Wimple's *eyes*, I treated my *boddy* very badly. I smoked as many cigarettes in an hour and a half as she did in a year. ("Miss Wimple, the doctors had a conference about that right in front of me; they agreed it isn't *good* for me, but they officially decided I should be left with one indulgence.") I constantly demanded ice cubes. Moreover I took drugs. ("Miss Wimple, they are what have been *prescribed*, for—")

But they were not Nature's Remedies, Miss Wimple patiently explained. Miss Wimple and Nature gave me a lot of trouble in those days; trouble which had by now been transmuted into the intellectual. Refined sugar was one of the Devil's instruments because honey was Nature's Sweetener. But everything was not that simple. After all, tobacco, alcohol and raw opium were Nature's Products, too, Miss Wimple; every one of them as vegetable as hell; springing from the Good Earth and making for human enjoyment with a minimum of processing intervention. . . .

No; it was not that; I had missed some point. There were, for example, vitamins. In the common man's pharmacopoeia, all vitamins are good, but in Miss Wimple's scale of values there were good vitamins and bad vitamins—and the bad vitamins were those that had been synthesized. Refinement, *si*; synthesis, *no*—was that it? *Almost*, except that refined sugar. . . . Oh, well.

III

He sat in the boxcar on the edge of the excited group of boys, wondering what all the fuss was about. They were all mustered around the three squat metal boxes that stood against the far side of the big canvas tent into which they had paid their pennies, and over the door of which hung a huge banner with big garish letters that read, "Picture Gallery." He had never been to a carnival before, and it thrilled him; the noise, the dust, the barrel-organs grinding out the gaudy music-hall tunes, the scarlet-ribboned monkeys clambering up the arms and shoulders of the tattered music-makers, squeaking madly and pelting the laughing audience with peanuts and banana skins; the brightly coloured tents with their Vanishing Lady and Madame Makura the fortune teller and the Smallest Man in the World; the huge catherine-wheels and chairoplanes whirling high overhead; the shooting galleries and lottery tents and the gay young girls screaming on the bumper cars in a raucous din and den of noise, their wide-flared summer dresses flung high by the onrush of air, the boys and young men laughing and winking and making obscene signs with their fingers. He had sat entranced by it all, his brothers pushing him in through the crowd with lusty yells of "Gangway!" and "Let us pass, mister!" and they they had found this "Picture Gallery" a good distance away

from all the other tents, almost on the edge of the large
field where the carnival was being held to help the local
church building funds. The scruffy-looking fellow on
the door had grinned at him and was about to make
some sly remark, but then smiled weakly when he
noticed that the boys were a tough-looking lot and
some of them very tall for their age. They had pushed
him into the dimness of the tent, and there he now sat,
quite forgotten, as the boys swarmed excitedly around
the queer-looking machine-like boxes from which
emanated a strange luminous green glow. The
machines had handles clamped onto the sides, which
the boys turned slowly as they looked down into the
opening at the top. Some of the boys were very quiet,
very intent, absorbed in watching; others whistled, and
howled, and slapped their thighs or the behinds of their
mates, with ribald cries of "Will you look at that!" and
"Look at the dollies on that wan!" Presently his big
brother came back, rubbing his eyes with his knuckles,
and looked down at him thoughtfully, then grinned
and pushed him in the boxcar up to one of the
machines.

"Jasus, no!" cried his eldest brother Jem, rushing
over in panic when he divined Tony's lewd intention,
his honest fat face showing real horror. "You can't
show them dirty pictures to a cripple!" The others all
laughed; Tony gave Jem a shove that sent him sprawl-
ing, then hoisted his crippled brother onto his
shoulder. From his perch on that broad promontory,
he could see inside the "picture box" quite clearly, and
he was amazed at what he saw. As Tony began to turn
and manipulate the control lever on the side, a whole
perfectly defined and delineated little world in
miniature began to flicker and blur and hover finally into focus upon the small square oblong screen that was

fixed to the luminous bottom of the box, the magic
Pandora box so humbly and unexpectedly hidden and
enclosed by four rusty metal sides. He was enchanted;
everything drifted away from the fringes of his
awareness and perception, and he was utterly absorbed in watching the marvellous fairytale microcosmic
world opening up before him. It was like being in the
local picturehouse on a Saturday afternoon—the
famous "Bower" as it was known locally, so typical of
local humour, since there was not a flower or shrub or
plant in sight; except here it was even better, more
engrossing, for here the screen was so small, and
everything so quiet, and the rowdy rude turmoil of the
audience so far away, that he alone was the spectator,
the sole looker-on as the little luminous performance
sprang into life on the little luminous screen, drawing
his mind downwards and onto it like a magnet.

A woman was preparing for bed; that is to say, she
was taking off her clothes one by one, quite slowly,
quite daintily, holding each skimpy garment delicately
by the tips of her fingers before dropping it out of sight,
which he fancied was the way people in foreign coun-
tries went to bed. She was a buxom, jolly-looking
young woman, who kept smiling and simpering to
herself, as if thinking of something funny, enjoying a
private joke. Her movements were dream-like, unhur-
ried, melodic, like a ballerina; every gesture she made
seemed to flow, to ripple as she swayed and floated
about the bedroom disrobing herself, peeling the black
silky garments from her pearly body with a slightly
unreal, self-conscious lassitude. Then to his annoyance
the picture shook, blurred, went out of focus; the
woman appeared too bunty, her head too large for the
rest of her, a Picasso-like distortion of reality that would
have amused him, only now he really wanted to see

the woman as she really was, for something strange was happening in his mind, or in some far corner of his mind; a certain memory was floating to the top, to the surface of his thoughts, but before he could grasp it, identify it, it darted away, back into the subterranean cave where such things remain hidden most of the time. Tony, still hoisting him easily on his shoulder, stopped joking with his mates long enough to steady the control handle and the picture resumed its normal perspective and proportions, enabling him, watching avidly, again to behold everything quite clearly and without interference.

The woman standing sideways; she was clad only in her black shift now, and her breasts thrust forward arrogantly. He started to sweat. Again, the memory hovered in his mind, tantalizing, tormenting; when, and where, and why had he felt like this before? The woman started to raise this silky sheath from her body, lifting it over her head; he saw the dimpled hollow at the base of her spine, over the curved buttocks...and he remembered.

There were six of them sleeping on the large straw mattress spread out on the floor in a corner of the back bedroom; his mother called it a "paliass," which made him laugh. It sounded like a friendly donkey. As usual, he had made sure to get a good position, wedged comfortably between two warm bodies, and he had been snug enough, until he woke up with a rotten smell in his nostrils. Someone had let off, and he knew who the culprit was, so he grabbed a hunk of Pete's behind and squeezed vigorously with his big toe and second toe, until Pete grunted and cursed roundly in his sleep and squirmed away. Mother said that the reason why Pete farted so much was that he had the "windy colic" and so she gave him more senna pods and "opening medicine" than the others. Saturday night was always senna pod night; they were supposed to be very good for the bowels, a part of the anatomy he could never quite locate or understand very clearly, except that they were somewhere in the belly and caused pains when he couldn't pass his motion in the lavatory. Therefore, to his mind, bowels were somehow mixed up with lavatory pots and he was always horrified in case one day he would look down into the depths of the pot and see, underneath him, the entangled mass of his bowels scoured from him by the force of the senna pod leaves he had taken. On account of his gusty habits of exhaling posterior air, they nick-named Pete "Windy," which sent Pete into a rage for it was also the name that people called cowards, though his brother could never be called that, for he spoke more often and more forcefully with his fists than with his mouth.

Saturday night was also the night when his eldest brother Jem came in steaming with porter. Jem was only starting to drink, just an apprentice at it but very willing to learn, and was not as used to it as their father, who made it his second profession. Their father had been drinking since he was twelve, when a pint of stout cost only a penny and a "half one" three-halfpence, so that he often got "locked" on a shilling which he earned as a messenger boy. Their father used to say that, instead of blood, he had alcohol running in his veins; that seemed very strange for he could fancy the whiskey and beer bubbling and hissing in his father's veins like red-hot lava, and he supposed it was this that made his father look and act so wild sometimes, his eyes bulging out as if they were on stalks and the lost wild look in them. But Jem was not quite eighteen yet, and drank secretly with his pals, in mortal dread of their father finding out, and so each Saturday night he stumbled and staggered up the stairs in his stockinged feet, maybe starting to hum a snatch of a song to himself before remembering their father in bed in the front bedroom, listening maybe, the heavy black belt on a chair by the bedside. This Saturday night was no exception; up came Jem, up the darkened stairs, holding his boots in one hand, feeling for the handrail with the other and puffing heavily with exertion and excess beer, hiccuping garrulously, excusing himself to himself, mumbling in a placating whispering soliloquy: "I'm not jarred, Pop—true as God I'm not—wouldn't do a thing like that—just a few jars, that's all—but not jarred, Pop—true as God. . . ." Jem made it, just made it, into the back room, before a sudden upheaval shook him and he barely got to the window in time before he emptied himself of all that black bileful porter—right on top of a prowling tomcat, damping that animal's amorous spirits. The cat fled squealing indignantly and shrilly. Jem fell back into the room and lay on his mouth and nose, in his good pressed suit, and mumbling and muttering something about taking the "pledge" in the morning, and soon he was snoring and whistling down his nose.

There was one good bed in the room, pushed into the far corner, in which the three older girls slept; two of them were already asleep, having washed themselves in the pantry behind a locked door, plaited their hair and cleaned their teeth and scraped the dirt from behind their finger and toe nails, for they were going to the altar in the morning to "receive," and their mother was very strict on going to God looking clean and neat and tidy. Lil, the very eldest, though only twenty or so, was "going steady" so the others said, and was not yet in; though she often got belted for staying out late, she was seldom in early, and even on the nights when she did not go out, she would sit below in the kitchen reading her romance novels and love magazines until all hours, until their father would shout down at her to come up to bed and stop wasting the light. He had seen her reading a big thick book the night before called *Gone With the Wind* which their mother said would bring the curse of God on the house because it was supposed to be dirty. He would have tried to steal a peep at it, but it was so big somebody was bound to see him, and anyhow he was only supposed to read his catechism just now in preparation for his confirmation. He found the catechism very boring, but his mother said it would make him holy. He read and read it, but never felt very holy. It probably meant floating on air or something like that, and that did not appeal to him, for he was sure he'd fall down with a bang.

He could never go to sleep very easily, and would lie awake in the night while the others snored and snored, thinking of many things, things he felt rather than saw, for there was not much to see from within the four rough wooden sides of the old boxcar, and there was not much to be seen from the front window either, except other houses facing, and buses, and cars, and the kids playing and running out in the streets. Sometimes there would be a great roar in the sky, and looking up, he would see an aeroplane passing, and he would watch it until it was just a dark speck in the distance and then nothing, and he would dream about that for hours, thinking of the people it was carrying inside it, so far up above the world, and how it could float on air like that, and where it might be going. He wanted to be inside a plane one day; he could imagine what it would be like, high over the clouds even, with green bits of the earth opening up between, and the whole sky in-

tensely blue and unbroken above. It would be like flying very near to God, he fancied, and if there was a
hole in the sky anywhere to be found, it might be possible to enter heaven just like that, like climbing in
through an unclosed window or a crack in the roof.
Maybe that was the only way most people ever got into
heaven—as burglars.

This night sleep would not come; he lay between
two of his brothers and wished himself to sleep, but it
would not come. Through the frayed lace curtains on
the window he could see the moon in the sky, shaped
like a silver half-crown, going under a large soft cloud
that was likewise frayed around its yellowish edges,
moving under the cloud like a strange-shaped fish
under water, or a form seen through smoked glass, a
pearly swan gliding elegantly in and out of cloudy reefs
and lagoons. He loved to watch the moon; he could
see the faint pencil markings on it, as if someone had
begun to draw something on its glowing surface, then
tired of the game and stopped. He would trace a sort of
pattern of the markings and make pictures of his own;
the moon reminded him of a big round frothy-white
bubble of milk swimming in a huge black-blue sea, and
the stars were the lesser bubbles in that same sea. He
discerned a very bright reddish star, quite close to the
moon, and as always he held himself rigid and began
to sweat, for it seemed only a matter of minutes before
the two would collide and set the sky on fire with a terrible bang. Sooner than watch, he ducked his head
quickly under the bedclothes and shut his eyes tight;
under there, all was pitch blackness, dense and thick,
pushing in upon his eyes, pressing upon the pupils,
making them ache, as if someone were rubbing their
knuckles against them. He prayed by the time he came
up for air the star would have passed the moon safely.

He slept; a deep, dreamless sleep, and when he awoke, hours or minutes later, his mind was quite clear, sharp, lucid, but quite empty of either thought or memory, without possessions, like a clear, bright, well-swept empty room. Into that clear emptiness hovered something soft and dark; as soft and dark and light as a leaf floating through the air, falling into his mind gently but clearly, sharply defined, finely etched against the luminous night sky outside; a form at the window. She stood there, a perfect silhouette, her arms upraised, her hair falling darkly down her back, her bare shoulders creamy in the moonlight; she sighed, stirred, as if she had been standing a long time at the window, gazing out; her dark-burning-silk slip hissed as she raised it over her head and sat down on the edge of the bed shadowed in the recess corner. Unable to draw away his eyes, held by something he did not understand but which hammered hotly inside him, he saw her reach behind with her hand, humming softly to herself; then, his whole body suddenly flaming and a loud roaring in his temples, he saw her pale breasts appear over the dark satian cupolas; she bent a little forward, putting away the bra, and her young breasts shone, the lace pattern of the curtains swaying on her flesh, the nipples dark as berries in snow; it was beauty, and perfection, and terror for him who watched in all the muteness and turmoil of his nature. She still hummed softly, happily, to herself, but above her quiet joyfulness, she caught the sound of his moan, as if from some deep pain, some animal distress; and moving swiftly, she came and knelt down on the floor beside where he lay, holding her dress up to her with one hand and feeling for his forehead with the other, stroking him gently, thinking he was having a bad dream. He did not dare look up; he could not swallow

the spit that lay burning like a bile in his throat; he cursed her fiercely in his mind to go away and leave him
alone. The next day, and for many days after that, he
could not look at his sister, or meet the puzzled enquiry
in her eyes, and he did not know why.

And so he remembered, as he looked at the woman
undressing on the miniature screen inside the circus
tent, where and when he had had those same painful,
ecstatic, guilty feelings, and the remembrance burned
in him, yet added a subtle zest, a delicious forbidden
excitement; the woman was taking the last silk sheath
from her body; a haze of anguish and pleasure swam
and danced before his eyes; the woman, now naked,
was slowly, slowly turning around....The screen
went dead, blank; his brother stopped turning the con-
trols and put him roughly down again into the boxcar.
The other boys stood about, not knowing where to
look, hands in pockets, whistling, trying to look as if
they had noticed nothing; his brother stood above him,
tall, resolute, strong-limbed and straight, and he hated
his brother just then, hated all those other so knowing
and so capable fools who had just witnessed his shame
and guilt, for they had made him conscious of these
emotions for the first time ever, and he felt soiled,
muddled. He wanted to lash out blindly and in rage; he
felt betrayed, felt the dagger-thrust of that betrayal
knife through him, and his hatred was the only clean
thing left in him now, the only clear, articulate thing left
in him, a white tide of violence roaring and soaring and
flaring to vivid life.

From *To Race the Wind*
Harold Krents

Petrarch had his Laura, Dante had his Beatrice, and I had my Susie Gritz. She entered my life shortly after our family moved out to Wading River for the summer.

On the afternoon after our arrival I sat alone on the beach.

My constant companion of summers past, Chris Marvel, was spending the first six weeks of the vacation visiting his grandparents in Kansas, and I looked forward to the summer with all the keen anticipation of a child about to receive a booster shot.

My reveries were interrupted by the voice of Ginny Korman.

"Come with me," she commanded imperiously, "I want to talk to you in private for a couple of minutes."

Ginny's family owned a house just a few steps from ours, and our parents were the best of friends. This cordiality, however, had never extended down to Ginny and me.

She belonged to a gang of kids, and summer after summer she had met my friendly advances with disdain.

Not even the valiant efforts of her mother, Florrie, had been able to soften Ginny's heart sufficiently to get her to work on my admittance into "The Gang."

So I had already reconciled myself to yet another summer of remaining the envious onlooker.

With a mixture of excitement and fear I obediently followed Ginny down the beach; excitement because she had actually deigned to notice my existence, and fear of what was about to unfold now that she finally had. The only thing sharper than Ginny's tongue was her fingernails, and several times over the previous summers I had seen both used to terrifying advantage upon my friend Chris.

I had no idea whether I was going to my salvation or my execution.

"Harold," she said condescendingly when she finally came to an abrupt halt, "for a long time now, you've wanted to join the gang. Well, I've just talked to all of them, and, to be perfectly honest, they don't like you very much at all."

"I don't really blame them," I said miserably.

"Neither do I," she replied.

A long silence followed, and I finally assumed that I was dismissed.

"Well," I said to her, "thanks for telling me, Ginny; it was really nice of you to talk to them."

"Don't mention it," she said.

I had taken four steps back in the direction from which I had come when my progress was again arrested by her command.

"Come back," she ordered sharply, "there's more."

I desperately wanted to keep right on going, to go off by myself and be alone. However, disobedience was positively unthinkable. Slowly, I turned around and came back to where she was standing to hear the conclusion of her depressing report.

"Even though I agree with them, I tried to reason with them. I said to them, 'Look, I know that Harold talks too much. I know that he tries too hard to be friendly, and that he'll make the summer miserable for us if we let him in, but my mother says that I have to try and get him in or she won't drive us to the movies even once during the whole summer.'"

"I bet the kids were really mad at you," I said sympathetically.

"What else could I do?" she asked desperately. "Without my mother driving, we'll never be able to go miniature golfing or get to the movies. I just had to try really hard to get you in, much as I hated to."

"What finally happened?" I asked breathlessly.

"After an awful lot of fighting, they finally agreed to let you come to the party I'm having at my house on Thursday night."

"You mean I'm actually part of the gang?"

"Well, we all agreed to try you out to see if there was any way that you could fit."

Perhaps it wasn't the most enthusiastic acceptance I have ever received, but it was acceptance nonetheless; and at that time in my lonely life, acceptance of any kind was a step up.

Five minutes after I arrived at Ginny's party, I was sorry that I had ever come. It had nothing to do with the welcome I received from the members of the gang. As a matter of fact, contrary to my fearful expectations, they were quite cordial to me. I learned it had a lot to do with the fact that my backer for permanent admission had noised it about among the group that my mother had a large station wagon and would be a willing driver to a multitude of summer diversions if I was accepted.

No, my sudden desire to be back home had to do exclusively with the proposed activity of the evening—Post Office.

Now, as far as I was concerned, girls were simply boys with higher voices. The prospect of an evening of enforced kissing bored me thoroughly. If belonging merely meant spending your time kissing some girl, then they could keep it.

Well, I would just have to suffer through it. The only problem was that I hadn't the vaguest idea of the rules of the game. However, I had no intention of communicating my ignorance to anyone.

"I'll be postmaster first," said Ginny.

The girls retired into another room from which occasional gigglings emanated.

Finally, Ginny came into the room where the boys were sitting and assigned each of us a number.

"Okay, which one of you wants to go first?" Ginny asked.

I had no idea about who wanted to go first, but I sure knew who wanted to go last. I did my very best to make myself as unobtrusive as possible. However, fate dictated otherwise.

"Since this is Harold's first time, let him go first," said Neil Brown expansively.

"Great idea, Neil," said Ginny enthusiastically.

I didn't have the vaguest idea of how to proceed, so I sat very quietly hoping for some inspiration.

"Well," said Ginny impatiently after a very long silence, "pick a number already."

"Don't rush me," I responded plaintively, and I sighed with relief at having escaped the embarrassment of having to admit that I had never played before.

"Number five," I cried out confidently.

"That's my number," said Michael Jampole, and the room reverberated with uproarious laughter. At that moment, I wished for a quick death.

"I just wanted to make sure that you were awake," I said to Michael when the laughter died down a bit.

"I had no idea you could be so funny," said Neil.

"What did I tell all of you," crowed Ginny delightedly.

"Number four," I said hopefully. I breathed easily when silence continued to reign throughout the room. However, a moment later, I was once more on the ropes in an agony of indecision.

"What kind of stamp do you want?" Ginny asked.

"I wonder if God has every played Post Office," I thought desperately. "If he hasn't, it wouldn't do much good to ask him to get me out of this." However, I sent up a quick, silent prayer nonetheless.

Apparently, He had played the game before because no laughter resounded after I whispered, "A three-cent stamp please."

Ginny disappeared, and a moment later she returned and ordered me to follow her.

We entered a third room, and Ginny disappeared immediately, leaving me alone with Susie Gritz.

"You're scared," she said.

"How can you tell?"

"Because you're all hunched over. Why are you scared?" she asked, and she moved rapidly across the room and patted me gently on the cheek.

"I'm scared because I've never played Post Office before, and I'll die if I do anything that's going to make people laugh at me," I blurted out.

I shall always be grateful to Susie for what she did next. With the gentleness of a woman twenty years old, instead of merely ten, she put her arms around me and kissed me on the mouth.

Suddenly, I knew what it was all about. In the split second that her lips touched mine, I made the discovery, which every male since Adam has made, that life could be very special and the thing that made it so special was females.

For a long time we clung to each other while strange, exquisite feelings ran through me. Yet none of them could have possibly been classified as desire. I was only eleven years old then, and she was just ten.

I was also overwhelmed with joy that into my lonely world had entered a person who seemed to be saying, "You really do matter, Harold Krents. It makes a real big difference whether you're happy, sad, scared, or lonely."

"You two are slowing the whole game up," said Ginny irritably as she reentered the room.

Susie and I slowly let go of each other, and I flew out of the room, leaving childhood behind me!

I never found out how to play Post Office, but somehow it didn't really matter. I knew her number and that was enough.

However, as the days passed, clouds began to gather on my horizon. Susie was a very pretty girl, and there were several other rivals for her affections, the most dangerous being Stuart Deutsch.

During the following weeks both of us attempted to win her.

She expressed a desire to learn Braille, having read the life of the founder of the system, Louis Braille.

Several afternoons were spent as I taught her how to read and write each combination of dots. I must admit that I made the system as confusing as possible in order to prolong the lessons for as long as I could.

I put my newly discovered song-writing ability to good use and composed an original song for her.

However, no matter how hard I racked my brain, the only words that I could come up with which rhymed with Gritz were tits and shits—neither of which were appropriate.

At last I hit upon the idea of working with her entire

name within the song without making it one of the rhyming words. I have forgotten the lyrics, but I can assure you that what they lacked in quality, they made up for in passion.

Susie's response to my lyrical love-making was even more enthusiastic than ever I had hoped. She swore undying devotion to me, accepted my ring, and I wallowed in triumph.

Tuesday, July 17, 1956, was a clear, hot day. I found Stuie on the beach for the first time since my stunning victory. Feeling that the conquerer must be gracious in victory, I chatted amicably with my rival for several minutes. As I was about to leave him, he said something which amused me.

"I'm really glad that you've taken it so well, Harold," Stuie said. "If Susie had liked you better than me, I would never have been so nice." I smiled to myself.

A little later two determined little boys confronted a very embarrassed ten-year-old girl and demanded to know which she really cared for the most.

With a sense of the dramatic that women are born with, Susie said, "I'll give the middle name of the one I really like most."

I was filled with quiet confidence just waiting for her to say "Eliot."

"Louis," Susie said—and my world came crashing all about me.

From *The Long Walk Home*

Leonard Kriegel

A few nights later I went on my first date. All that day, I had anticipated going. It was another test, but this time there was another person. My will might not be enough. It wasn't sex that I wanted, not then. For sex was still so deep a fear then that all I could do was to verbalize a manhood I was searching for, to talk as if I had already made it, to shroud that ultimate fear in a certain new boldness of approach. I was frightened of dating. It was that simple. For I didn't know what was expected of me. And I had already noted the wary faces of mothers eyeing me from hotel porches, faces that said, "Keep away from my daughter. She's not for you, sonny. She's not for you. Not that I want to hurt you, but. . . ."

That night I met Barbara in front of the movie theater on the town's main street. A flight of wooden steps led up to the theater's entrance, an easy flight to walk up, for there were banisters on both sides. But I delayed going up for as long as possible. Somehow, I had to persuade Barbara to walk in front of me, to force this pleasant, well-curved girl of sixteen to clear a way for my embarrassment. Her presence disturbed me. She was simply too much the thing I wanted, the gold star that had been awarded to me in the third grade, the beacon toward which I struggled, however fearfully, in this reach for selfhood. My success in swimming the lake didn't matter; it wasn't going to help me tonight. "Walk ahead of me," I demanded.

"Why?"

I didn't answer her. I couldn't. But she walked up ahead of me, evidently not thinking the request strange, or else so unmoved by what to her was a mechanical thing, a date, that its strangeness didn't disturb her. I followed her up those stairs as quickly as I could, aware of her eyes on my back that somehow had disappeared by the time I reached the top and turned around. But that only made it worse; that meant not that the eyes didn't exist but only that they were trying to trick me into believing that they didn't exist. Shrewd and intent as I was, I would create an enemy of the world even if it chose to proclaim its indifference toward me.

In the dark of the theater, I underwent a change I had expected. That image on the screen severed me from the outside world, and I was again free to indulge my Hollywood-primed memory, only this time with another person. It was easy enough to "cop my feel," to glue my hand to the softness of her flesh and coat my awkwardness with the mannerisms of the experienced stud. I drifted into the tempo of the film and sought with my hands to create a communion of seekers. Barbara was willing, all too willing to inexperienced hands that belonged to a mind that worried about the cripple in me. Throughout the movie, the voice that rose from that mind whispered, "Doesn't she know you're crippled? Doesn't she know about the legs?" Whether she knew or not didn't matter; what mattered was that I knew, as I had known while dressing on the dock. That was my secret, a burdensome secret that I could share with no one else, for to no one else could it have any real meaning.

When the picture finally ended, only my hands had been fulfilled. The rest of me was burning with shame as the lights went on and we stood up to leave. I expected Barbara to slap my face, turn on her heel, and leave the theater, true to a virtue she had never claimed and would not have known what to do with. But all she did was smile and coo something like, "Wasn't it a lovely picture?" And wasn't it, whatever it had been.

I didn't have to ask Barbara to walk down the stairs ahead of me. That wasn't necessary now. For, not having been slapped, my hands tingled with the feel of her softness, and visions in the Hollywood style drifted like overly ripe clouds through my head. Soft lights, music, the thread of violins, the rich taste of halvah. Lord, I was a lover!

We spent the next half hour in the drug store, sipping sodas along with the other mating children who were all around us. And how thrilled I was to number myself among them. Our talk was child's talk, some of her, some of me. I didn't even listen very attentively, for I was gearing myself for the long walk back to her hotel, which was at the south end of the lake, about three quarters of a mile from where we were. Her mother entered the luncheonette, nodded abruptly to Barbara, and left. "That's my mother," Barbara said brightly. She was being very informative.

I had already exaggerated my success in the darkened movie theater, and now I wanted to leave the drug store, to squeeze her softness once again, to permit my body, made edgier and bolder, some new, more probing success. It turned out to be an unfortunate consequence of discovering that I was not so far outside the society of my peers as I had believed. "Listen," I said, "I'll take you home now. It's after eleven.".

"It's a long walk," Barbara answered doubtfully.

"I'll take you," I insisted, for her tone had turned it into a conscious battle again. And again I was the prover, and what could I prove so surely as this new manhood springing up within me.

We got up and left the luncheonette. The night was cool and sharp, the stars burning into a protean expanse that made me think of nothing but my own hugeness—my arms pushing me forward, like unstoppable pistons, until I had almost forgotten the girl at my side in the clean rush of security surging through my soul. Because I was what I was, a giant making giant strides through night's darkness. A crippled giant. I thought of what I had read somewhere about Steinmetz, that hunchback mechanic playing with the world's illusion, pouring all his own frustration into the inventive toys needed by General Electric. Or was it General Motors? It didn't matter, did it? Did Steinmetz or Spinoza or F.D.R. or anyone hungry for the body's fulfillment, did any of them matter as long as I was a giant?

My euphoria lasted only for as long as we walked across that dark curving country road. Every time the lights from some onrushing car gashed the thin line of blue-black where trees and sky fused together, Barbara and I dropped off to the side of the road. My energy was all that existed for me, even as I kissed her, and all I was capable of admiring was this self, from which, in the intensity of my love, I almost felt detached—my self was making its own way through the rich blackness and I was no more, really, than an onlooker. Then we were standing in front of the lawn of Barbara's hotel. The moment was awkward, but Barbara was reassuring. Soft in the shadows, she took my right hand and placed it on her breast. I felt delighted, triumphant, new-sprung, and I suddenly thought of throwing her down here, on the lawn in front of the hotel. It was a dramatic thought, and as I pulled her close to me I could think of nothing but what a great lover I was destined to become. I kissed her hard, and then, with a quiet grace all my own, I fell down.

It was as if the ground had sprung up to meet me, insisting on my giving it the final victory of the night. I lay there, face pressed to the grass, kissing the grass where I had expected to be kissing only Barbara, for the moment amused by this latest trick, this vicious shrewdness, of the enemy. And Barbara, too, that beautiful bundle of softness which had been meant for me, only for me and for this night, Barbara was equally amused. Not that she laughed or giggled, as I suppose I expected her to; her voice, in fact, was taut with the serious, the lofty, the dignified, as she asked, "Are you all right?"

"Sure," I answered. "Sure, I'm all right."

"What happened?"

"I tripped. I guess I tripped."

"You're sure you're all right."

"Yes." I pushed myself up on my hands, and, leaning on my right hand alone, I said, "Give me the crutches."

Barbara picked up the crutches. She had a certain sure dignity of touch that gagged me for the moment, holding the crutches as if they were not wooden crutches but rather spears, clean and agile and shafted in their ability to pierce flesh. I knew little enough about the terror of the phallus then but it was with me for sure. This was my potency, my strength; like Samson's hair, this was the feeder of my manhood. I pushed straight, using one crutch handle to boost myself, then grabbing the other crutch from Barbara's hand. "It could have happened to anyone," Barbara offered in a whisper, and with that I suddenly hated her, not for trying to soothe my pain but for transforming it from pain to absurdity, from taking that which was mine alone and playing with it as if my life were some common universal accident. And then, stepping on the pieces with all the goodness that she had been taught by Flatbush spinsters, she added, "I'll see you tomorrow."

"I'll see you," I answered, the words thick on my tongue. "I'll see you."

I watched her walk up the path to the hotel. She moved well, conscious of her body's curves. I hated her even more for moving so well. She paused just before she disappeared into the hotel. I took a few more breaths, then turned away. I began the walk back to my own hotel.

The strength had been drained from my body. . . . I huddled in the shadows of the trees each time I heard the roar of a car engine, afraid that if I were offered a lift I would accept. And I had to go on by myself, for now the enemy had the upper hand. Now the night, the sky, the roar of the motorboat cruising the pitch-black lake, the mysterious sudden noises that I heard from the side of the road, all were mocking me. "Submit!" the noises cried. "Submit to that which we know you are!" I walked on, and suddenly I was crying, crying with the sheer rage that had been burning within me ever since I took that fall, crying because the fever in the blood was now no more than the desire not to be humiliated any further, crying because I had come so close to the greatest and most necessary of all the incestuous loves, the love of the self, only to have it wrenched from my grasp.

Finally I was standing on the porch of my hotel. There was no one else around, and all of the lights but one had been turned off. I leaned against the wall and lit a cigarette. The night was still clear, the moon and the plethora of stars glaring sharply through the blackness. "You bastards," I whispered tearfully. "I'll get you still, you bastards. You just see if I don't." And with that I went into my room, burning with fever.

It was almost noon when I awoke. The room was hot, a humid, sticky heat. My mouth felt dry and parched. I moved sluggishly, feverishly. I didn't go into town. All afternoon I just sat on the porch, watching the old women who made that porch their summer headquarters rocking back and forth, thinking of how I had crawled the night before as I had not crawled in a long time. I was different today, different both physically and psychologically. My edge had been honed. I had slipped away from my own consciousness and once again had made the world my measuring rod. All day long I wanted to curse and cry, and I fought this only because I was intimidated by the people around me. The world was rancid with the smell of my disease.

Late that afternoon, Barbara came up to the hotel. She greeted me brightly, as if the fall had never happened. She had a great deal of poise and compassion for a sixteen-year-old girl, but I lacked everything that afternoon except the memory of what had happened the night before. And I blamed her for that, spreading my intense self-pity until it coated the entire world. I baited Barbara, quite deliberately, and eventually her better nature was twisted out of shape until she began to cut into me. "Don't worry," she concluded, as she walked off the porch, "I'll see you again . . . in the city."

Flannery O'Connor

Besides the neutral expression that she wore when she was alone, Mrs. Freeman had two others, forward and reverse, that she used for all her human dealings. Her forward expression was steady and driving like the advance of a heavy truck. Her eyes never swerved to left or right but turned as the story turned as if they followed a yellow line down the center of it. She seldom used the other expression because it was not often necessary for her to retract a statement, but when she did, her face came to a complete stop, there was an almost imperceptible movement of her black eyes, during which they seemed to be receding, and then the observer would see that Mrs. Freeman, though she might stand there as real as several grain sacks thrown on top of each other, was no longer there in spirit. As for getting anything across to her when this was the case, Mrs. Hopewell had given it up. She might talk her head off. Mrs. Freeman could never be brought to admit herself wrong on any point. She would stand there and if she could be brought to say anything, it was something like, "Well, I wouldn't of said it was and I wouldn't of said it wasn't," or letting her gaze range over the top of the kitchen shelf where there was an assortment of dusty bottles, she might remark, "I see you ain't ate many of them figs you put up last summer."

They carried on their most important business in the kitchen at breakfast. Every morning Mrs. Hopewell got up at seven o'clock and lit her gas heater and Joy's. Joy was her daughter, a large blonde girl who had an artificial leg. Mrs. Hopewell thought of her as a child though she was thirty-two years old and highly educated. Joy would get up while her mother was eating and lumber into the bathroom and slam the door, and before long, Mrs. Freeman would arrive at the back door. Joy would hear her mother call, "Come on in," and then they would talk for a while in low voices that were indistinguishable in the bathroom. By the time Joy came in, they had usually finished the weather report and were on one or the other of Mrs. Freeman's daughters, Glynese or Carramae, Joy called them Glycerin and Caramel. Glynese, a redhead, was eighteen and had many admirers; Carramae, a blonde, was only fifteen but already married and pregnant. She could not keep anything on her stomach. Every morning Mrs. Freeman told Mrs. Hopewell how many times she had vomited since the last report.

Mrs. Hopewell liked to tell people that Glynese and Carramae were two of the finest girls she knew and that Mrs. Freeman was a *lady* and that she was never ashamed to take her anywhere or introduce her to anybody they might meet. Then she would tell how she happened to hire the Freemans in the first place and how they were a godsend to her and how she had had them four years. The reason for her keeping them so long was that they were not trash. They were good country people. She had telephoned the man whose name they had given as a reference and he had told her that Mr. Freeman was a good farmer but that his wife was the nosiest woman ever to walk the earth. "She's got to be into everything," the man said. "If she don't get there before the dust settles, you can bet she's dead, that's all. She'll want to know all your business. I can stand him real good," he had said, "but me nor my wife neither could have stood that woman one more minute on this place." That had put Mrs. Hopewell off for a few days.

She had hired them in the end because there were no other applicants but she had made up her mind beforehand exactly how she would handle the woman. Since she was the type who had to be into everything, then, Mrs. Hopewell had decided, she would not only let her be into everything, she would *see to it* that she was into everything—she would give her the responsibility of everything, she would put her in charge. Mrs. Hopewell had no bad qualities of her own but she was able to use other people's in such a constructive way that she never felt the lack. She had hired the Freemans and she had kept them four years.

Nothing is perfect. This was one of Mrs. Hopewell's favorite sayings. Another was: that is life! And still another, the most important, was: well, other people have their opinions too. She would make these statements, usually at the table, in a tone of gentle insistence as if no one held them but her, and the large hulking Joy, whose constant outrage had obliterated every expression from her face, would stare just a little to the side of her, her eyes icy blue, with the look of someone who has achieved blindness by an act of will and means to keep it.

When Mrs. Hopewell said to Mrs. Freeman that life was like that, Mrs. Freeman would say, "I always said so myself." Nothing had been arrived at by anyone that had not first been arrived at by her. She was quicker than Mr. Freeman. When Mrs. Hopewell said to her after they had been on the place a while, "You know, you're the wheel behind the wheel," and winked, Mrs. Freeman had said, "I know it. I've always been quick. It's some that are quicker than others."

"Everybody is different," Mrs. Hopewell said.

"Yes, most people is," Mrs. Freeman said.

"It takes all kinds to make the world."

"I always said it did myself."

The girl was used to this kind of dialogue for breakfast and more of it for dinner; sometimes they had it for supper too. When they had no guest they ate in the kitchen because that was easier. Mrs. Freeman always managed to arrive at some point during the meal and to watch them finish it. She would stand in the doorway if it were summer but in the winter she would stand with one elbow on top of the refrigerator and look down on them, or she would stand by the gas heater, lifting the back of her skirt slightly. Occasionally she would stand against the wall and roll her head from side to side. At no time was she in any hurry to leave. All this was very trying on Mrs. Hopewell but she was a woman of great patience. She realized that nothing is perfect, and that in the Freemans she had good country people and that if, in this day and age, you get good country people, you had better hang onto them.

She had plenty of experience with trash. Before the Freemans she had averaged one tenant family a year. The wives of these farmers were not the kind you would want to be around you for very long. Mrs. Hopewell, who had divorced her husband long ago, needed someone to walk over the fields with her; and when Joy had to be impressed for these services, her remarks were usually so ugly and her face so glum that Mrs. Hopewell would say, "If you can't come pleasantly, I don't want you at all," to which the girl, standing square and rigid-shouldered with her neck thrust slightly forward, would reply, "If you want me, here I am—LIKE I AM."

Mrs. Hopewell excused this attitude because of the leg (which had been shot off in a hunting accident when Joy was ten). It was hard for Mrs. Hopewell to realize that her child was thirty-two now and that for more than twenty years she had had only one leg. She thought of her still as a child because it tore her heart to think instead of the poor stout girl in her thirties who had never danced a step or had any *normal* good times. Her name was really Joy but as soon as she was twenty-one and away from home, she had had it legally changed. Mrs. Hopewell was certain that she had thought and thought until she had hit upon the ugliest name in any language. Then she had gone and had the beautiful name, Joy, changed without telling her mother until after she had done it. Her legal name was Hulga.

When Mrs. Hopewell thought the name, Hulga, she thought of the broad blank hull of a battleship. She would not use it. She continued to call her Joy to which the girl responded but in a purely mechanical way.

Hulga had learned to tolerate Mrs. Freeman who saved her from taking walks with her mother. Even Glynese and Carramae were useful when they occupied attention that might otherwise have been directed at her. At first she had thought she could not stand Mrs. Freeman for she had found that it was not possible to be rude to her. Mrs. Freeman would take on strange resentments and for days together she would be sullen but the source of her displeasure was always obscure; a direct attack, a positive leer, blatant ugliness to her face—these never touched her. And without warning one day, she began calling her Hulga.

She did not call her that in front of Mrs. Hopewell who would have been incensed but when she and the girl happened to be out of the house together, she would say something and add the name Hulga to the end of it, and the big spectacled Joy-Hulga would scowl and redden as if her privacy had been intruded upon. She considered the name her personal affair. She had arrived at it first purely on the basis of its ugly sound and then the full genius of its fitness had struck her. She had a vision of the name working like the ugly sweating Vulcan who stayed in the furnace and to whom, presumably, the goddess had to come when called. She saw it as the name of her highest creative act. One of her major triumphs was that her mother had not been able to turn her dust into Joy, but the greater one was that she had been able to turn it herslf into Hulga. However, Mrs. Freeman's relish for using the name only irritated her. It was as if Mrs. Freeman's beady steel-pointed eyes had penetrated far enough behind her face to reach some secret fact. Something about her seemed to fascinate Mrs. Freeman and then one day Hulga realized that it was the artificial leg. Mrs. Freeman had a special fondness for the details of secret infections, hidden deformities, assaults upon children. Of diseases, she preferred the lingering or incurable. Hulga had heard Mrs. Hopewell give her the details of the hunting accident, how the leg had been literally blasted off, how she had never lost consciousness. Mrs. Freeman could listen to it any time as if it had happened an hour ago.

When Hulga stumped into the kitchen in the morning (she could walk without making the awful noise but she made it—Mrs. Hopewell was certain—because it was ugly-sounding), she glanced at them and did not speak. Mrs. Hopewell would be in her red kimono with her hair tied around her head in rags. She would be sitting at the table, finishing her breakfast and Mrs. Freeman would be hanging by her elbow outward from the refrigerator, looking down at the table. Hulga always put her eggs on the stove to boil and then stood over them with her arms folded, and Mrs. Hopewell would look at her—a kind of indirect gaze divided between her and Mrs. Freeman—and would think that if she would only keep herself up a little, she wouldn't be so bad looking. There was nothing wrong with her face that a pleasant expression wouldn't help. Mrs. Hopewell said that people who looked on the bright side of things would be beautiful even if they were not.

Whenever she looked at Joy this way, she could not help but feel that it would have been better if the child had not taken the Ph.D. It had certainly not brought her out any and now that she had it, there was no more excuse for her to go to school again. Mrs. Hopewell thought it was nice for girls to go to school to have a good time but Joy had "gone through." Anyhow, she would not have been strong enough to go again. The doctors had told Mrs. Hopewell that with the best of care, Joy might see forty-five. She had a weak heart. Joy had made it plain that if it had not been for this condition, she would be far from these red hills and good country people. She would be in a university lecturing to people who knew what she was talking about. And Mrs. Hopewell could very well picture her there, looking like a scarecrow and lecturing to more of the same. Here she went about all day in a six-year-old skirt and a yellow sweat shirt with a faded cowboy on a horse embossed on it. She thought this was funny; Mrs. Hopewell thought it was idiotic and showed simply that she was still a child. She was brilliant but she didn't have a grain of sense. It seemed to Mrs. Hopewell that every year she grew less like other people and more like herself—bloated, rude, and squint-eyed. And she said such strange things! To her own mother she had said—without warning, without excuse, standing up in the middle of a meal with her face purple and her mouth half full—"Woman! do you ever look inside? Do you ever look inside and see what you are *not*? God!" she had cried sinking down again and staring at her plate, "Malebranche was right: we are not our own light. We are not our own light!" Mrs. Hopewell had no idea to this day what brought that on. She had only made the remark, hoping Joy would take it in, that a smile never hurt anyone.

The girl had taken the Ph.D. in philosophy and this left Mrs. Hopewell at a complete loss. You could say, "My daughter is a nurse," or "My daughter is a schoolteacher," or even, "My daughter is a chemical engineer." You could not say, "My daughter is a philosopher." That was something that had ended with the Greeks and Romans. All day Joy sat on her neck in a deep chair, reading. Sometimes she went for walks but she didn't like dogs or cats or birds or flowers or nature or nice young men. She looked at nice young men as if she could smell their stupidity.

One day Mrs. Hopewell had picked up one of the books the girl had just put down and opening it at random, she read, "Science, on the other hand, has to assert its soberness and seriousness afresh and declare that it is concerned solely with what-is. Nothing—how can it be for science anything but a horror and a phantasm? If science is right, then one thing stands firm: science wishes to know nothing of nothing. Such is after all the strictly scientific approach to Nothing. We know it by wishing to know nothing of Nothing." These words had been underlined with a blue pencil and they worked on Mrs. Hopewell like some evil incantation in gibberish. She shut the book quickly and went out of the room as if she were having a chill.

This morning when the girl came in, Mrs. Freeman was on Carramae. "She thrown up four times after supper," she said, "and was up twice in the night after three o'clock. Yesterday she didn't do nothing but ramble in the bureau drawer. All she did. Stand up there and see what she could run up on."

"She's got to eat," Mrs. Hopewell muttered, sipping her coffee, while she watched Joy's back at the stove. She was wondering what the child had said to the Bible salesman. She could not imagine what kind of a conversation she could possibly have had with him.

He was a tall gaunt hatless youth who had called yesterday to sell them a Bible. He had appeared at the door, carrying a large black suitcase that weighted him so heavily on one side that he had to brace himself against the door facing. He seemed on the point of collapse but he said in a cheerful voice. "Good morning, Mrs. Cedars!" and set the suitcase down on the mat. He was not a bad-looking young man though he had on a bright blue suit and yellow socks that were not pulled up far enough. He had prominent face bones and a streak of sticky-looking brown hair falling across his forehead.

"I'm Mrs. Hopewell," she said.

"Oh!" he said, pretending to look puzzled but with his eyes sparkling, "I saw it said 'The Cedars' on the mailbox so I thought you was Mrs. Cedars!" and he burst out in a pleasant laugh. He picked up the satchel and under cover of a pant, he fell forward into her hall. It was rather as if the suitcase had moved first, jerking him after it. "Mrs. Hopewell!" he said and grabbed her hand. "I hope you are well!" and he laughed again and then all at once his face sobered completely. He paused and gave her a straight earnest look and said, "Lady, I've come to speak of serious things."

"Well, come in," she muttered, none too pleased because her dinner was almost ready. He came into the parlor and sat down on the edge of a straight chair and put the suitcase between his feet and glanced around the room as if he were sizing her up by it. Her silver gleamed on the two sideboards; she decided he had never been in a room as elegant as this.

"Mrs. Hopewell," he began, using her name in a way that sounded almost intimate, "I know you believe in Chrustian service."

"Well, yes," she murmured.

"I know," he said and paused, looking very wise with his head cocked on one side, "that you're a good woman. Friends have told me."

Mrs. Hopewell never liked to be taken for a fool. "What are you selling?" she asked.

"Bibles," the young man said and his eye raced around the room before he added, "I see you have no family Bible in your parlor, I see that is the one lack you got!"

Mrs. Hopewell could not say, "My daughter is an atheist and won't let me keep the Bible in the parlor." She said, stiffening slightly, "I keep my Bible by my bedside." This was not the truth. It was in the attic somewhere.

"Lady," he said, "the word of God ought to be in the parlor."

"Well, I think that's a matter of taste," she began. "I think. . . ."

"Lady," he said, "for a Chrustian, the word of God ought to be in every room in the house besides in his heart. I know you're a Chrustian because I can see it in every line of your face."

She stood up and said, "Well, young man, I don't want to buy a Bible and I smell my dinner burning."

He didn't get up. He began to twist his hands and looking down at them, he said softly, "Well lady, I'll tell you the truth—not many people want to buy one nowadays and besides, I know I'm real simple. I don't know how to say a thing but to say it. I'm just a country boy." He glanced up into her unfriendly face. "People like you don't like to fool with country people like me!"

"Why!" she cried, "good country people are the salt of the earth! Besides, we all have different ways of doing, it takes all kinds to make the world go 'round. That's life!"

"You said a mouthful," he said.

"Why, I think there aren't enough good country people in the world!" she said, stirred. "I think that's what's wrong with it!"

His face had brightened. "I didn't inraduce myself," he said. "I'm Manley Pointer from out in the country around Willohobie, not even from a place, just from near a place."

"You wait a minute," she said. "I have to see about my dinner." She went out to the kitchen and found Joy standing near the door where she had been listening.

"Get rid of the salt of the earth," she said, "and let's eat."

Mrs. Hopewell gave her a pained look and turned the heat down under the vegetables. "*I* can't be rude to anybody," she murmured and went back into the parlor.

He had opened the suitcase and was sitting with a Bible on each knee.

"You might as well put those up," she told him. "I don't want one."

"I appreciate your honesty," he said. "You don't see any more real honest people unless you go way out in the country."

"I know," she said, "real genuine folks!" Through the crack in the door she heard a groan.

"I guess a lot of boys come telling you that they're working their way through college," he said, "but I'm not going to tell you that. Somehow," he said, "I don't want to go to college. I want to devote my life to Chrustian service. See," he said, lowering his voice, "I got this heart condition. I may not live long. When you know it's something wrong with you and you may not live long, well then, lady. . . ." He paused, with his mouth open, and stared at her.

He and Joy had the same condition! She knew that her eyes were filling with tears but she collected herself quickly and murmured, "Won't you stay for dinner? We'd love to have you!" and was sorry the instant she heard herself say it.

"Yes mam," he said in an abashed voice, " I would sher love to do that!"

Joy had given him one look on being introduced to him and then throughout the meal had not glanced at him again. He had addressed several remarks to her, which she had pretended not to hear. Mrs. Hopewell could not understand deliberate rudeness, although she lived with it, and she felt she had always to overflow with hospitality to make up for Joy's lack of courtesy. She urged him to talk about himself and he did. He said he was the seventh child of twelve and that his father had been crushed under a tree when he himself was eight year old. He had been crushed very badly, in fact, almost cut in two and was practically not recognizable. His mother had got along the best she could by hard working and she had always seen that her children went to Sunday School and that they read the Bible every evening. He was now nineteen year old and he had been selling bibles for four months. In that time he had sold seventy-seven bibles and had the promise of two more sales. He wanted to become a missionary because he thought that was the way you could do most for people. "He who losest his life shall find it," he said simply and he was so sincere, so genuine and earnest that Mrs. Hopewell would not for the world have smiled. He prevented his peas from sliding onto the table by blocking them with a piece of bread which he later cleaned his plate with. She could see Joy observing sidewise how he handled his knife and fork and she saw too that every few minutes, the boy would dart a keen appraising glance at the girl as if he were trying to attract her attention.

After dinner Joy cleared the dishes off the table and disappeared and Mrs. Hopewell was left to talk with him. He told her again about his childhood and his father's accident and about various things that had happened to him. Every five minutes or so she would stifle a yawn. He sat for two hours until finally she told him she must go because she had an appointment in town. He packed his Bibles and thanked her and prepared to leave, but in the doorway he stopped and wrung her hand and said that not on any of his trips had he met a lady as nice as her and he asked if he could come again. She had said she would always be happy to see him.

Joy had been standing in the road, apparently looking at something in the distance, when he came down the steps toward her, bent to the side with his heavy valise. He stopped where she was standing and confronted her directly. Mrs. Hopewell could not hear what he said but she trembled to think what Joy would say to him. She could see that after a minute Joy said something and that then the boy began to speak again, making an excited gesture with his free hand. After a minute Joy said something else at which the boy began to speak once more. Then to her amazement, Mrs. Hopewell saw the two of them walk off together, toward the gate. Joy had walked all the way to the gate with him and Mrs. Hopewell could not imagine what they had said to each other, and she had not yet dared to ask.

Mrs. Freeman was insisting upon her attention. She had moved from the refrigerator to the heater so that Mrs. Hopewell had to turn and face her in order to seem to be listening. "Glynese gone out with Harvey Hill again last night," she said. "She had this sty."

"Hill," Mrs. Hopewell said absently, "is that the one who works in the garage?"

"Nome, he's the one that goes to chiropractor school," Mrs. Freeman said. "She had this sty. Been had it two days. So she says when he brought her in the other night, he says, 'Lemme get rid of that sty for you,' and she says, "'How?' and he says, 'You just lay yourself down acrost the seat of that car and I'll show you." So she done it and he popped her neck. Kept on a-popping it several times until she made him quit. This morning," Mrs. Freeman said, "she ain't got no sty. She ain't got no traces of a sty."

"I never heard of that before," Mrs. Hopewell said.

"He ast her to marry him before the Ordinary," Mrs. Freeman went on, "and she told him she wasn't going to be married in no *office*."

"Well, Glynese is a fine girl," Mrs. Hopewell said. "Glynese and Carramae are both fine girls."

"Carramae said when her and Lyman was married Lyman said it sure felt sacred to him. She said he said he wouldn't take five hundred dollars for being married by a preacher."

"How much would he take?" the girl asked from the stove.

"He said he wouldn't take five hundred dollars," Mrs. Freeman repeated.

"Well we all have work to do," Mrs. Hopewell said.

"Lyman said it just felt more sacred to him," Mrs. Freeman said. "The doctor wants Carramae to eat prunes. Says instead of medicine. Says them cramps is coming from pressure. You know where I think it is?"

"She'll be better in a few weeks," Mrs. Hopewell said.

"In the tube," Mrs. Freeman said. "Else she wouldn't be as sick as she is."

Hulga had cracked her two eggs into a saucer and was bringing them to the table along with a cup of coffee that she had filled too full. She sat down carefully and began to eat, meaning to keep Mrs. Freeman there by questions if for any reason she showed an inclination to leave. She could perceive her mother's eye on her. The first round-about question would be about the Bible salesman and she did not wish to bring it on. "How did he pop her neck?" she asked.

Mrs. Freeman went into a description of how he had popped her neck. She said he owned a '55 Mercury but that Glynese said she would rather marry a man with only a '36 Plymouth who would be married by a preacher. The girl asked what if he had a '32 Plymouth and Mrs. Freeman said what Glynese had said was a '36 Plymouth.

Mrs. Hopewell said there were not many girls with Glynese's common sense. She said what she admired in those girls was their common sense. She said that reminded her that they had had a nice visitor yesterday, a young man selling Bibles. "Lord," she said, "he bored me to death but he was so sincere and genuine I couldn't be rude to him. He was just good country people, you know," she said, "—just the salt of the earth."

"I seen him walk up," Mrs. Freeman said, "and then later—I seen him walk off," and Hulga could feel the slight shift in her voice, the slight insinuation, that he had not walked off alone, had he? Her face remained expressionless but the color rose into her neck and she seemed to swallow it down with the next spoonful of egg. Mrs. Freeman was looking at her as if they had a secret together.

"Well, it takes all kinds of people to make the world go 'round," Mrs. Hopewell said. "It's very good we aren't all alike."

"Some people are more alike than others," Mrs. Freeman said.

Hulga got up and stumped, with about twice the noise that was necessary, into her room and locked the door. She was to meet the Bible salesman at ten o'clock at the gate. She had thought about it half the night. She had started thinking of it as a great joke and then she had begun to see profound implications in it. She had lain in bed imagining dialogues for them that were insane on the surface but that reached below to depths that no Bible salesman would be aware of. Their conversation yesterday had been of this kind.

He had stopped in front of her and had simply stood there. His face was bony and sweaty and bright, with a little pointed nose in the center of it, and his look was different from what it had been at the dinner table. He was gazing at her with open curiosity, with fascination, like a child watching a new fantastic animal at the zoo, and he was breathing as if he had run a great distance to reach her. His gaze seemed somehow familiar but she could not think where she had been regarded with it before. For almost a minute he didn't say anything. Then on what seemed an insuck of breath, he whispered, "You ever ate a chicken that was two days old?"

The girl looked at him stonily. He might have just put this question up for consideration at the meeting of a philosophical association. "Yes," she presently replied as if she had considered it from all angles.

"It must have been mighty small!" he said triumphantly and shook all over with little nervous giggles, getting very red in the face, and subsiding finally into his gaze of complete admiration, while the girl's expression remained exactly the same.

"How old are you?" he asked softly.

She waited some time before she answered. Then in a flat voice she said, "Seventeen."

His smiles came in succession like waves breaking on the surface of a little lake. "I see you got a wooden leg," he said. "I think you're brave. I think you're real sweet."

The girl stood blank and solid and silent.

"Walk to the gate with me," he said. "You're a brave sweet little thing and I liked you the minute I seen you walk in the door."

Hulga began to move forward.

"What's your name?" he asked, smiling down on the top of her head.

"Hulga," she said.

"Hulga," he murmured, "Hulga. Hulga. I never heard of anybody name Hulga before. You're shy, aren't you, Hulga?" he asked.

She nodded, watching his large red hand on the handle of the giant valise.

"I like girls that wear glasses," he said. "I think a lot.

I'm not like these people that a serious thought don't ever enter their heads. It's because I may die."

"I may die too," she said suddenly and looked up at him. His eyes were very small and brown, glittering feverishly.

"Listen," he said, "don't you think some people was meant to meet on account of what all they got in common and all? Like they both think serious thoughts and all?" He shifted the valise to his other hand so that the hand nearest her was free. He caught hold of her elbow and shook it a little. "I don't work on Saturday," he said. "I like to walk in the woods and see what Mother Nature is wearing. O'er the hills and far away. Pic-nics and things. Couldn't we go on a pic-nic tomorrow? Say yes, Hulga," he said and gave her a dying look as if he felt his insides about to drop out of him. He had even seemed to sway slightly toward her.

During the night she had imagined that she seduced him. She imagined that the two of them walked on the place until they came to the storage barn beyond the two back fields and there, she imagined, that things came to such a pass that she very easily seduced him and that then, of course, she had to reckon with his remorse. True genius can get an idea across even to an inferior mind. She imagined that she took his remorse in hand and changed it into a deeper understanding of life. She took all his shame away and turned it into something useful.

She set off for the gate at exactly ten o'clock, escaping without drawing Mrs. Hopewell's attention. She didn't take anything to eat, forgetting that food is usually taken on a picnic. She wore a pair of slacks and a dirty white shirt, and as an afterthought, she had put some Vapex on the collar of it since she did not own any perfume. When she reached the gate no one was there.

She looked up and down the empty highway and had the furious feeling that she had been tricked, that he had only meant to make her walk to the gate after the idea of him. Then suddenly he stood up, very tall, from behind a bush on the opposite embankment. Smiling, he lifted his hat which was new and wide-brimmed. He had not worn it yesterday and she wondered if he had bought it for the occasion. It was toast-colored with a red and white band around it and was slightly too large for him. He stepped from behind the bush still carrying the black valise. He had on the same suit and the same yellow socks sucked down in his shoes from walking. He crossed the highway and said, "I knew you'd come!"

The girl wondered acidly how he had known this. She pointed to the valise and asked, "Why did you bring your Bibles?"

He took her elbow, smiling down on her as if he could not stop. "You can never tell when you'll need the word of God, Hulga," he said. She had a moment in which she doubted that this was actually happening and then they began to climb the embankment. They went down into the pasture toward the woods. The boy walked lightly by her side, bouncing on his toes. The valise did not seem to be heavy today; he even swung it. They crossed half the pasture without saying anything and then, putting his hand easily on the small of her back, he asked softly, "Where does your wooden leg join on?"

She turned an ugly red and glared at him and for an instant the boy looked abashed. "I didn't mean you no harm," he said. "I only meant you're so brave and all. I guess God takes care of you."

"No," she said, looking forward and walking fast, "I don't even believe in God."

At this he stopped and whistled. "No!" he exclaimed

as if he were too ashamed to say anything else.

She walked on and in a second he was bouncing at her side, fanning with his hat. "That's very unusual for a girl," he remarked, watching her out of the corner of his eye. When they reached the edge of the wood, he put his hand on her back again and drew her against him without a word and kissed her heavily.

The kiss, which had more pressure than feeling behind it, produced that extra surge of adrenalin in the girl that enables one to carry a packed trunk out of a burning house, but in her, the power went at once to the brain. Even before he released her, her mind, clear and detached and ironic anyway, was regarding him from a great distance, with amusement but with pity. She had never been kissed before and she was pleased to discover that it was an unexceptional experience and all a matter of the mind's control. Some people might enjoy drain water if they were told it was vodka. When the boy, looking expectant but uncertain pushed her gently away, she turned and walked on, saying nothing as if such business, for her, were common enough.

He came along panting at her side, trying to help her when he saw a root that she might trip over. He caught and held back the long swaying blades of a thorn vine until she had passed beyond them. She led the way and he came breathing heavily behind her. Then they came out on a sunlit hillside, sloping softly into another one a little smaller. Beyond, they could see the rusted top of the old barn where the extra hay was stored.

The hill was sprinkled with small pink weeds. "Then you ain't saved?" he asked suddenly, stopping.

The girl smiled. It was the first time she had smiled at him at all. "In my economy," she said, "I'm saved and you are damned but I told you I didn't believe in God."

Nothing seemed to destroy the boy's look of admiration. He gazed at her now as if the fantastic animal at the zoo had put its paw through the bars and given him a loving poke. She thought he looked as if he wanted to kiss her again and she walked on before he had the chance.

"Ain't there somewheres we can sit down sometime?" he murmured, his voice softening toward the end of the sentence.

"In that barn," she said.

They made for it rapidly as if it might slide away like a train. It was a large two-story barn, cool and dark inside. The boy pointed up the ladder that led into the loft and said, "It's too bad we can't go up there."

"Why can't we?" she asked.

"Yer leg," he said reverently.

The girl gave him a contemptuous look and putting both hands on the ladder, she climbed it while he stood below, apparently awestruck. She pulled herself expertly through the opening and then looked down at him and said, "Well, come on if you're coming," and he began to climb the ladder, awkwardly, bringing the suitcase with him.

"We won't need the Bible," she observed.

"You never can tell," he said, panting. After he had got into the loft, he was a few seconds catching his breath. She had sat down in a pile of straw. A wide sheath of sunlight, filled with dust particles, slanted over her. She lay back against a bale, her face turned away, looking out the front opening of the barn where hay was thrown from a wagon into the loft. The two pink-speckled hillsides lay back against a dark ridge of woods. The sky was cloudless and cold blue. The boy dropped down by her side and put one arm under her and the other over her and began methodically kissing her face, making little noises like a fish. He did not remove his hat but it was pushed far enough back not to interfere. When her glasses got in his way, he took them off her and slipped them into his pocket.

The girl at first did not return any of the kisses but presently she began to and after she had put several on his cheek, she reached his lips and remained there, kissing him again and again as if she were trying to draw all the breath out of him. His breath was clear and sweet like a child's and the kisses were sticky like a child's. He mumbled about loving her and about knowing when he first seen her that he loved her, but the mumbling was like the sleepy fretting of a child being put to sleep by his mother. Her mind, throughout this, never stopped or lost itself for a second to her feelings. "You ain't said you loved me none," he whispered finally, pulling back from her. "You got to say that."

She looked away from him off into the hollow sky and then down at a black ridge and then down farther into what appeared to be two green swelling lakes. She didn't realize he had taken her glasses but this landscape could not seem exceptional to her for she seldom paid any close attention to her surroundings.

"You got to say it," he repeated. "You got to say you love me."

She was always careful how she committed herself. "In a sense," she began, "if you use the word loosely, you might say that. But it's not a word I use. I don't have illusion. I'm one of those people who see *through* to nothing."

The boy was frowning. "You got to say it. I said it and you got to say it," he said.

The girl looked at him almost tenderly. "You poor baby," she murmured. "It's just as well you don't understand," and she pulled him by the neck, face-down, against her. "We are all damned," she said, "but some of us have taken off our blindfolds and see that there's nothing to see. It's a kind of salvation."

The boy's astonished eyes looked blankly through the ends of her hair. "Okay," he almost whined, "but do you love me or don'tcher?"

"Yes," she said and added, "in a sense. But I must tell you something. There mustn't be anything dishonest between us." She lifted his head and looked him in the eye. "I am thirty years old," she said. "I have a number of degrees."

The boy's look was irritated but dogged. "I don't care," he said. "I don't care a thing about what all you done. I just want to know if you love me or don'tcher?" and he caught her to him and wildly planted her face with kisses until she said, "Yes, yes."

"Okay then," he said, letting her go. "Prove it."

She smiled, looking dreamily out on the shifty landscape. She had seduced him without even making up her mind to try. "How?" she asked, feeling that he should be delayed a little.

He leaned over and put his lips to her ear. "Show me where your wooden leg joins on," he whispered.

The girl uttered a sharp little cry and her face instantly drained of color. The obscenity of the suggestion was not what shocked her. As a child she had sometimes been subject to feelings of shame but education had removed the last traces of that as a good surgeon scrapes for cancer; she would no more have felt it over what he was asking than she would have believed in his Bible. But she was as sensitive about the artificial leg as a peacock about his tail. No one ever touched it but her. She took care of it as someone else would his soul, private and almost with her own eyes turned away. "No," she said.

"I known it," he muttered, sitting up. "You're just playing me for a sucker."

"Oh no no!" she cried. "It joins on at the knee. Only at the knee. Why do you want to see it?"

The boy gave her a long penetrating look. "Because," he said, "it's what makes you different. You ain't like anybody else."

She sat staring at him. There was nothing about her face or her round freezing-blue eyes to indicate that this had moved her; but she felt as if her heart had stopped and left her mind to pump her blood. She decided that for the first time in her life she was face to face with real innocence. This boy, with an instinct that came from beyond wisdom, had touched the truth about her. When after a minute, she said in a hoarse high voice, "All right," it was like surrendering to him completely. It was like losing her own life and finding it again, miraculously, in his.

Very gently he began to roll the slack leg up. The artificial limb, in a white sock and brown flat shoe, was bound in a heavy material like canvas and ended in an ugly jointure where it was attached to the stump. The boy's face and his voice were entirely reverent as he uncovered it and said, "Now show me how to take it off and on."

She took it off for him and put it back on again and then he took it off himslf, handling it as tenderly as if it were a real one. "See!" he said with a delighted child's face. "Now I can do it myself!"

"Put it back on," she said. She was thinking that she would run away with him and that every night he would take the leg off and every morning put it back on again. "Put it back on," she said.

"Not yet," he murmured, setting it on its foot out of her reach. "Leave it off for a while. You got me instead."

She gave a little cry of alarm but he pushed her down and began to kiss her again. Without the leg she felt entirely dependent on him. Her brain seemed to have stopped thinking altogether and to be about some other function that it was not very good at. Different expressions raced back and forth over her face. Every now and then the boy, his eyes like two steel spikes, would glance behind him where the leg stood. Finally she pushed him off and said, "Put it back on me now."

"Wait," he said. He leaned the other way and pulled the valise toward him and opened it. It had a pale blue spotted lining and there were only two Bibles in it. He took one of these out and opened the cover of it. It was hollow and contained a pocket flask of whiskey, a pack of cards, and a small blue box with printing on it. He laid these out in front of her one at a time in an evenly-spaced row, like one presenting offerings at the shrine of a goddess. He put the blue box in her hand. THIS PRODUCT TO BE USED ONLY FOR THE PREVENTION OF DISEASE, she read, and dropped it. The boy was unscrewing the top of the flask. He stopped and pointed, with a smile, to the deck of cards. It was not an ordinary deck but one with an obscene picture on the back of each card. "Take a swig," he said, offering her the bottle first. He held it in front of her, but like one mesmerized, she did not move.

Her voice when she spoke had an almost pleading sound. "Aren't you," she murmured, "aren't you just good country people?"

The boy cocked his head. He looked as if he were just beginning to understand that she might be trying to insult him. "Yeah," he said, curling his lips slightly, "but it ain't held me back none. I'm as good as you any day in the week."

"Give me my leg," she said.

He pushed it farther away with his foot. "Come on

now, let's begin to have us a good time," he said coaxingly. "We ain't got to know one another good yet."

"Give me my leg!" she screamed and tried to lunge for it but he pushed her down easily.

"What's the matter with you all of a sudden?" he asked, frowning as he screwed the top on the flask and put it quickly back inside the Bible. "You just a while ago said you didn't believe in nothing. I thought you was some girl!"

Her face was almost purple. "You're a Christian!" she hissed. "You're a fine Christian! You're just like them all—say one thing and do another. You're a perfect Christian, you're...."

The boy's mouth was set angrily. "I hope you don't think," he said in a lofty indignant tone, "that I believe in that crap! I may sell Bibles but I know which end is up and I wasn't born yesterday and I know where I'm going!"

"Give me my leg!" she screeched. He jumped up so quickly that she barely saw him sweep the cards and the blue box into the Bible and throw the Bible into the valise. She saw him grab the leg and then she saw it for an instant slanted forlornly across the inside of the suitcase with a Bible at either side of its opposite ends. He slammed the lid shut and snatched up the valise and swung it down the hole and then stepped through himself.

When all of him had passed but his head, he turned and regarded her with a look that no longer had any admiration in it. "I've gotten a lot of interesting things," he said. "One time I got a woman's glass eye this way. And you needn't to think you'll catch me because Pointer ain't really my name. I use a different name at every house I call at and don't stay nowhere long. And I'll tell you another thing, Hulga," he said, using the name as if he didn't think much of it, "you ain't so smart. I been believing in nothing ever since I was born!" and then the toast-colored hat disappeared down the hole and the girl was left, sitting on the straw in the dusty sunlight. When she turned her churning face toward the opening, she saw his blue figure struggling successfully over the green speckled lake.

Mrs. Hopewell and Mrs. Freeman, who were in the back pasture, digging up onions, saw him emerge a little later from the woods and head across the meadow toward the highway. "Why, that looks like that nice dull young man that tried to sell me a bible yesterday," Mrs. Hopewell said, squinting. "He must have been selling them to the Negroes back in there. He was so simple," she said, "but I guess the world would be better off if we were all that simple."

Mrs. Freeman's gaze drove forward and just touched him before he disappeared under the hill. Then she returned her attention to the evil-smelling onion shoot she was lifting from the ground. "Some can't be that simple," she said. "I know I never could."

From *Cancer Ward*

Alexander Solzhenitsyn

Dyomka was lying in a tiny double room. His neighbor had been discharged and he was expecting a new one to arrive the next day from the operating theater. Meanwhile he was alone.

A week had passed, and with it had gone the first agony of his amputated leg. The operation was receding into the past, but his leg stayed with him torturing him as if it hadn't been removed. He could feel each toe separately.

Dyomka was delighted to see Oleg and greeted him like an elder brother. Of course they were like relatives, those friends of his from his former ward. Some of the women patients had sent him food too; there it was on his bedside table under a napkin. None of the new arrivals could come and visit him or bring him anything.

Dyomka was lying on his back nursing his leg (or rather what remained of a leg, less than a thigh), still with his huge turban-shaped bandage. But his head and arms were free.

"Well, hello, Oleg, how are you?" he said, taking Oleg's hand in his. "Sit down, tell me how things are in the ward."

The upstairs ward he'd recently left was the world he was used to. Here, downstairs, the nurses and the orderlies were different and so was the routine. There was constant bickering about who had to do what.

"Well, what can you expect in the ward...?" Oleg was looking at Dyomka's yellowed face. It seemed whittled, as if grooves had been planed in his cheeks. His eyebrows, nose and chin had been planed down and sharpened. "It's still the same."

"Is 'Personnel' still there?"

"Oh yes. 'Personnel's' there."

"What about Vadim?"

"Vadim's not too good. They didn't get the gold. And they're frightened of secondaries."

Dyomka frowned his concern in a way that made Vadim his junior. "Poor fellow," he said.

"So, Dyomka, you ought to thank God they amputated yours in time."

"I could still get secondaries."

"Oh, I don't think so."

But who could tell? Even doctors, how could they detect whether the solitary, destructive cells had or hadn't stolen through the darkness like landing craft, and where they had berthed?

"Are they giving you X rays?"

"They roll me in on a small cart."

"You've got a clear road ahead now, my friend. You must get better and get used to using a crutch."

"No, it'll have to be two. Two crutches."

Poor boy, he'd already thought of everything. Even in the old days he'd frowned like a grown man. Now he seemed to have grown even older.

"Where are they going to make them for you? Right here?"

"Yes, in the orthopedic wing."

"They'll be free of charge, at least?"

"Well, I've made an application. What have I got to pay with?"

They sighed. The sighs came easily from them, two men who year in, year out had had very little to cheer them.

"How are you going to finish school next year, then?"

"I'll finish or bust."

"What'll you live on? You can't work in a factory now."

"They've promised me a disability rating. I don't know if it'll be Group 2 or Group 3."

"Which one is Group 3, then?" asked Kostoglotov. He didn't understand these disability groups, or any other civil regulations for that matter.

"It's one of these groups—enough to buy you bread, but not enough for sugar."

He was a real man, Dyomka, he'd thought of everything.

The tumor was trying hard to sink him, but he was still steering his course.

"Will you go to the university?"

"I'll do my best."

"You'll study literature?"

"That's it."

"Listen to me, Dyomka, I'm talking seriously, you'll just ruin yourself. Why don't you work on radio sets? It's a quiet life, and you can always earn something on the side."

"Oh, to hell with radio sets!" Dyomka blinked. "Truth is what I love."

"Well, you can repair radio sets and tell the truth at the same time, you old fool!"

They couldn't agree. They argued it this way and that. They talked about Oleg's problems as well. That was another grown-up thing about Dyomka, he was interested in others. Normally, youth is only concerned with itself. Oleg spoke to him about his own situation as he might to an adult.

"Oh, that's awful. . ." Dyomka mumbled.

"I don't reckon you'd change places with me, would you?"

"G-g-god knows."

The upshot of it all was that, what with the X rays and the crutches, Dyomka would have to spend another six weeks lounging about the hospital. He would get his discharge in May.

"Where will you go first?"

"I'll go straight to the zoo," said Dyomka, cheering up. He'd already spoken to Oleg several times about this zoo. They would stand together on the clinic porch and Dyomka would describe exactly where the zoo was, how it was lurking over there, across the river, behind those thick trees. He had spent years reading about animals and listening to stories about them on the radio, but he had never actually seen a fox or a bear, let alone a tiger or an elephant. He had always lived in places where there was no menagerie, circus or forest. His cherished dream was to go out and meet the animals, and it was a dream that did not fade as he grew older. He expected something extraordinary from this encounter. On the very day he'd come to hospital with his aching leg, the first thing he'd done was visit the zoo, only it happened to be the one day of the week it was closed. "Listen, Oleg," he said, "you will be discharged soon, won't you?"

Oleg sat there, hunching his back. "Yes, I expect so. My blood won't take any more. The nausea's wearing me out."

"But you will go to the zoo, won't you?" Dyomka couldn't let the matter go. He would have thought the worse of Oleg otherwise.

"Yes, I may."

"No, you must. I'm telling you, you must go! And you know what? Send me a postcard afterwards, will you? It'll be easy enough for you, and it'll give me such pleasure. Write and tell me what animals they have now and which is the most interesting, all right? Then I'll know a month before they let me out. You will go, won't you? And write to me? They say they have crocodiles and lions and. . . ."

Oleg promised.

He left the room to go and lie down himself, leaving Dyomka alone in the small room with the door closed. For a long time Dyomka didn't pick up his book, he just looked at the ceiling and through the window, and thought. He couldn't see anything through the window. Its bars converged into one corner and it looked out on a nondescript corner of the yard bounded by the wall of the Medical Center. There was not even a strip of direct sunlight on the wall now. But it wasn't an overcast day either. The sun was slightly veiled, not completely covered by clouds, and gave out a sort of diffused, angular light. It must have been one of those dullish days, not too hot and not too bright, when Spring was doing her work without undue fuss or noise.

Dyomka lay motionless, thinking pleasant thoughts: how he'd learn to walk on crutches, briskly and smartly; how one really summery day shortly before May Day he'd go out and explore the zoo from morning until the evening train; how he'd have plenty of time now to get quickly though his subjects at school and do well and read all the essential books he'd hitherto missed. There would be no more wasted evenings with the other boys, going off to a dance hall after tormenting himself about whether to go or not, even though he couldn't dance away. No more of that. He would just turn on his light and work at his books.

There was a knock at the door.

"Come in," said Dyomka.

(Saying "Come in" gave him a feeling of satisfaction. He had never known a situation where people had to knock at his door before entering.)

The door was flung open, letting in Asya.

Asya came in, or rather burst in. She rushed into the room as though someone was chasing her, pushed the door shut behind her and stood there by the door, one hand on the knob, the other holding the front of her dressing gown together.

She was no longer the Asya who had dropped in for a "three-day checkup," who was expected back in a few days' time by her track friends at the winter stadium. She had sagged and faded. Even her yellow hair, which couldn't change as quickly as the rest of her, hung down pitifully now.

She was wearing the same dressing gown, an unpleasant one without buttons that had covered many shoulders and been boiled in goodness knows what boilers. It looked more becoming on her now than before.

Asya looked at Dyomka and her eyelashes trembled a little. Had she come to the right place? Would she have to rush on somewhere else?

She was utterly crushed now. No longer Dyomka's senior by a full year in school, she had lost her advantage of extra experience, her knowledge of life and the three long journeys she had made. She seemed to Dyomka almost like part of him. He was very pleased to see her. "Asya, sit down! What's the matter?" he said.

They had had many talks together in hospital. They had discussed his leg (Asya had come out firmly against giving it up). After the operation she had come to see him twice, brought him apples and cookies.

Natural though their friendship had been that first evening, it had since then become even more so. And she'd told him, although not all at once, exactly what was wrong with her. She had had a pain in her right breast, they had found some sort of hard lumps in it, they were giving her X-ray treatment for it and making her put pills under her tongue.

"Sit down, Asya. Sit down."

She let go of the doorknob and walked a few steps to the stool at the head of Dyomka's bed, dragging her hand behind her along the door, along the wall. It was as though she had to hold onto them and grope her way.

She sat down.

She sat down, and she didn't look Dyomka in the eye. She looked past him at the blanket. She wouldn't turn to face him, and he couldn't twist his body round to see her directly either.

"Come on now, what's the matter?" He had to play the "older man" again, that was his role. He threw his head back, craning his neck over the pile of pillows so that he could see her, still lying on his back.

Her lip trembled. Her eyelashes fluttered.

"As-asyenka!" Dyomka just had time to say the word. He was overcome with pity for her, he wouldn't have dared call her "Asyenka" otherwise. Suddenly she threw herself onto his pillow, her head against his, her little sheaf of hair tickling his ear.

"Please, Asyenka!" he begged her, fumbling over the blanket for her hand. But he couldn't see her hands and so he didn't find it.

She sobbed into the pillow.

"What is it? Come on, tell me, what is it?"

But he'd almost guessed what it was.

"They're going to c-c-cut it off . . .!"

She cried and she cried. And then she started to groan, "O-o-oh."

Dyomka couldn't remember ever hearing such a long-drawn-out moan of grief, such an extraordinary sound, as this "O-o-oh."

"Maybe they won't do it after all," he said, trying to soothe her. "Maybe they won't have to." But he knew somehow that his words wouldn't be enough to comfort her sorrow.

She cried and cried into his pillow. He could feel the place beside him; it was already quite wet.

Dyomka found her hand and began to stroke it. "Asyenka," he said, "maybe they won't have to."

"They will, they will! They're going to do it on Friday..."

And she let out such a groan that it transfixed Dyomka's soul.

He couldn't see her tear-stained face. A few locks of hair found their way through to his eyes. It was soft hair, soft and ticklish.

Dyomka searched for words, but they wouldn't come. All he could do was clasp her hand tighter and tighter to try to stop her. He had more pity for her than he had ever had for himself.

"What have I got to live for?" she sobbed.

Dyomka's experiences, vague as they were, provided him with an answer to this question, but he couldn't express it. Even if he could have done, Asya's groan was enough to tell him that neither he, nor anyone, nor anything at all would be able to convince her. Her own experience led to only one conclusion: there was nothing to live for now.

"Who in the world will w-w-want me n-n-now?" She stumbled the words out inconsolably. "Who in the world...?"

She buried her face in his pillow once again. Dyomka's cheek was now quite wet.

"Well, you know." He was still trying to soothe her, still clasping her hand. "You know how people get married . . . They have the same sort of opinions . . . the same sort of characters. . . ."

"What sort of fool loves a girl for her character?" She started up angrily, like a horse rearing. She pulled her hand away, and Dyomka saw her face for the first time—wet, flushed, blotched, miserable and angry. "Who wants a girl with one breast? Who wants a girl like that? When she's seventeen!" She shouted the words at him. It was all his fault.

He didn't know how to console her.

"How will I be able to go to the beach?" she shrieked, as a new thought pierced her. "The beach! How can I go swimming?" Her body corkscrewed, then crumpled. Her head clutched between her hands, she slumped down from Dyomka toward the floor.

Unbearably, she began to imagine bathing suits in different styles—with or without shoulder straps, one-piece or two-piece, every contemporary and future fashion, bathing suits in orange and blue, crimson and the hue of the sea, in one color or striped with scalloped edges, bathing suits she hadn't yet tried on but had examined in front of a mirror—all the ones she would never buy and never wear.

She could never show herself on the beach again. It had suddenly struck her as the most excruciating, the most mortifying fact of her existence. Living had lost all meaning, and this was the reason why.

Dyomka mumbled something clumsy and inept from his pile of pillows. "Of course, you know, if no one will have you. . .Well, of course, I realize what sort of a man I am now. . .But I'll always be happy to marry you, you know that. . ."

"Listen to me, Dyomka!" A new thought had stung Asya. She stood up, faced him and looked straight at him. Her eyes were wide open and tearless. "Listen to me, you'll be the last one! You're the last one who can see it and kiss it. No one but you will ever kiss it! Dyomka, *you* at least must kiss it, if nobody else!"

She pulled her dressing gown apart (it wasn't holding together anyway). It seemed to him that she was weeping and groaning again as she pulled down the loose collar of her nightdress to reveal her doomed right breast.

It shone as though the sun had stepped straight into the room. The whole ward seemed on fire. The nipple glowed. It was larger than he had ever imagined. It stood before him. His eyes could not resist its sunny rosiness.

Asya brought it close to his face and held it for him.

"Kiss it! Kiss it!" she demanded. She stood there, waiting.

And breathing in the warmth her body was offering him, he nuzzled it with his lips like a suckling pig, gratefully, admiringly. Nothing more beautiful than this gentle curve could ever be painted or sculptured. Its beauty flooded him. Hurriedly his lips took in its even, shapely contour.

"You'll remember?. . . You'll remember, won't you? You'll remember it was there, and what it was like?" Asya's tears kept dropping onto his close-cropped head.

When she did not take it away, he returned to its rosy glow again and again, softly kissing the breast. He did what her future child would never be able to do. No one came in, and so he kissed and kissed the marvel hanging over him.

Today it was a marvel. Tomorrow it would be in the trash bin.

From *Ordinary Daylight*
Andrew Potok

During the first couple of months at St. Paul's I didn't much want to go home for weekends, even though everyone else in our group went. I felt cozy where I was and feared the discomfort and threat, even with my own family, of sighted, "normal," life and expectations. On those weekends at St. Paul's I practiced cane travel, listened to my tapes of C. Wright Mills's *The Marxists* or Rudolf Arnheim's *Visual Thinking*, studied braille, typed, did exercises on a broken-down stationary bicycle in the cellar. I ate alone or with some of the old people at St. Raphael's, which housed the geriatric blind. If friends came to visit, I'd have a coffee or drink off the property with them and impatiently hurry back to the Center alone, explaining that I had unfinished work there. I knew I'd be back in the real world soon enough.

Sometimes, over the weekends I spent at St. Paul's, Katie would call from a noisy bar in Fall River or Providence. In these drunken, sexy calls, she would attempt to describe in her gravelly whisky voice what we might be doing together at that very moment if either she were back at the Center or I were with her in the bar. As the weekends came to an end, I would eagerly await everyone's return, especially Katie's. She would usually be brought back in a long black Cadillac that stopped right in front of the arched entrance. A small heavy man with black wavy hair would get out slowly from the driver's seat, walk around the car, help Katie out, and walk her inside. She wore her most sedate clothes for these occasions: heels, stockings, a little furry animal around her neck. The short man would lead her by her elbow, help her into a chair in the lobby, deposit her overnight bag under the rack of coats near the door to the women's quarters, and, without turning toward her again, walk back to his car and drive away. She sat for a while, listening to who was present, and if she heard my voice, she'd ask for a Coke. She later told me that her companion was Frankie.

"Oh, yeah? Who's Frankie?" I asked.

"You know," she said. "Frankie. I told you about Frankie. He's the big man in the area."

Katie was the only one in our group who was completely blind. She saw nothing, not light, not shadow. Not only were her optic nerves totally cut in two, but some months after, recovering from the accident, she walked, eyes first, into the prongs of a wall telephone and had, she confided to me toward the end of our stay at St. Paul's, two prosthetic glass eyes.

My feelings of belonging were undermined by the people who sometimes came, unannounced, to visit me during the week. Each person in our closely knit group had come to represent a heroic struggle, victory over overwhelming odds, a frightening and sorrowful tale. But when we were seen as a group by an outsider, I felt us as inmates in a grotesque zoo, institutionalized freaks in an asylum. When visitors entered the portals of our weird institution, they saw Little Fred groping, a hand extended in front of his face, fluttering his inoperative eyes uncontrollably, defending himself with each step against some hidden enemy. As he moved, his jerky motions, his suspicious sweeps of an area with his cane or his hand, his fitful starts and sideways detours conveyed not the assured student of a new independence but a confused macho swagger gone wrong. Or these visitors saw lovely Margie rising from her chair to smack into a half-opened door or to be snarled up, like a fish in a net, among a rack full of hanging coats. To an outsider, these scenes were confusing and wrong, unseemly, even shocking. Seeing one stumbling blind person has its own tension and fascination, I thought, but intruding on a herd of us, bumping into one another, into walls and doors, tripping over canes, seemed to me like kicking over a rock to find a bunch of albino lemmings scurrying for cover.

When my friends Pat and Paul, who lived nearby, came once or twice a week to read aloud to me, I made sure to wait for them outside. The moment they got out of their car, I whisked them through the lobby and down the stairs into the basement, where we sat among the clattering pipes, sipping the bottle of Scotch they sometimes brought. Over the four months of my stay in Newton, we read all of Kropotkin aloud.

After one very busy day, crammed full of mobility, braille, shop, Cristofanetti's videation, and the technique of daily living, I went to bed early and was falling asleep to the Cavatina of Beethoven's Thirteenth Quartet when I heard a crash and loud voices downstairs. Katie was back from Howard Johnson's, and she was lusciously, wantonly drunk. I heard my name. I heard the canes hanging on a rack near the front door hit heavily, making a sound like distant firecrackers. One of the standing ashtrays fell with a thud and rolled grittily down the lineoleum floor. "Andy, where are you, you son of a bitch?" I heard her wail. Ray was with her, and I felt sure that he would quiet her and put her to bed. But Ray wasn't doing well either. He growled and groaned and hit the wall with a terrible thump. When he, a diabetic, was that drunk, it usually meant trouble. He caromed off the walls of the stairwell going up, fell into bed, and began to snore heavily.

"Wait up, you bastard," Katie yelled as she reached the door leading upstairs to the men's dormitory. "Where the fuck is Andy?" she bellowed as the hydraulic closer slammed the door to the stairwell shut behind her. She stood silently for a moment. No one answered. Then I heard the *whoosh* of her cane. It smacked the wall hard. She was furious; furious for not seeing, for feeling horny, for being denied the pleasures of the eyes. We were all furious about that. "Come on, baby, let's do it," she said. "Say something, goddamn it!" She began to climb the stairs, the cane bouncing behind.

My reactions came from the gut, as true and primitive as if I had met a hungry bear in the woods. I was scared and, God help me, repelled. Not because we were seven men in a small space, almost on top of one another. Not because I had qualms about being with women other than Charlotte. Not because Katie was unattractive. She was soft and round and wonderfully loose. I gulped for breath. I was repelled because she was blind. I wanted to scream with the horror of this revelation. I wanted to push myself, scratch out my own eyes.

I turned to the wall and tried to stop breathing. I was absolutely still. Little Fred, in the bed next to mine, whispered, "Hey Andy, you want me to stop her?"

"Tell her I'm not here," I murmured.

"What?" Fred asked.

"I'm not here."

He stood up in his shorts and felt around for his pants. Katie had reached the top step, panting and muttering: "Come on, baby." Fred was now in the hall, trying to deal with her. "Not you, you son of a bitch," she howled.

"He's not here," Fred said. "He's out. Away for the night."

"Bullshit," Katie roared.

"He's gone," Fred said, and then he whispered in her ear and she smacked him with her handbag. Then they were both on Fred's bed, and I heard the rustle of clothes and soft curses.

The door downstairs slammed again, and heavy footsteps came up the stairs. Snyder, the nighttime supervisor, there to help the diabetics in case of emergency, stumbled drunkenly up. Big and gawky and grubby, Snyder walked into a night he would never forget.

Fred and Katie untangled easily. He escorted her to the women's dormitory, where she knocked the toilet off its moorings, flooding the downstairs. He put the toilet back together only to be yanked away to deal with Ray, who was convulsing with a serious insulin reaction. It seemed the Day of Judgment had come. In the convulsion, the deluge, the upheaval, I stood in my shorts, full of self-loathing and shame. Horrified, I witnessed Ray being carried out on a stretcher. His jaws were clamped shut and all his muscles rigid. He was handed down the stairs, making incomprehensible gurgling noises. They brought him back a day later, his chemistry fixed for the moment, ready again to drown his fear and anger.

Katie never talked about that night. When, a few days later, someone spoke of her apocalyptic binge, she said: "I guess I really tied one on."

I didn't recover, not really, for a very long time. It turned out to be a matter of years before blindness—hers, mine, all of ours—became, quite simply, the inability to see with our eyes, nothing more. But as I faced the wall that night, trying not to breathe, I saw only scooped out, rotting sockets, decay everywhere, and heard horrendous sounds, like fish eyes popping in a hot oven.

From *Heartsounds*

Martha Weinman Lear

He knelt in the center of the big bed, seemingly lost in some fine fit of passion. Surreptitiously he checked his pulse. Not with his fingers to the wrist. Nothing so vulgar. Just a hand resting casually at his throat, up there against the carotid artery, so that it would look as though he were simply, in the gallant old way, supporting his weight on his elbows.

His pulse was a little fast, but nothing worrisome. Good, so far. He was sweating. But it was the hot sweat of exercise, not the clammy sweat of shock. He was panting. But it was normal enough to pant. His heart was pounding. Oh, damn, pounding very hard now. But that was normal too. Wasn't it?

That was the trouble. How could he be sure? How could you tell a heart that pounded toward orgasm from a heart that pounded toward its own destruction? No *petit mal*, that.

Better rest a moment. Catch my breath. But smoothly, gracefully, so that she will not suspect. It would be terrible if she knew how scared I am. The thing would be ruined for her.

This was rich. Not to laugh aloud, but funny. Maybe some day, if he survived this sweet fearsome screw, he would get up the courage to tell about it in his lecture. The lecture called "Sexual Aspects of Medical Practice," which he had given so many times, with such success, to audiences of doctors.

"...Now, as to the sexual aspects of heart disease, we know that twenty-four percent of coronary patients are impotent sexually, although there is no physiological basis for it. Why should such a large group be impotent?

"The most obvious reason is the fear that they may overexert themselves and die in the act of sex. But beyond that, there is the psychological association of a heart attack with loss of symbolic potency. The cardiac is no longer the hard-driving money earner, no longer the weight lifter; no longer the macho man; his self-image is devastated and he loses his potency....

"We know from nurses in the intensive-care units that there is a very high incidence of masturbation among the male cardiac patients. Here, too, evidence of anxiety....

"In studying the impotent group, we find that over ninety percent of their doctors never mentioned sex during convalescence...important to understand the role we ourselves may play in perpetuating the patient's fears....When discussing resumption of physical activity, important to discuss sex....Emphasize that there is no need to be afraid...

"Now, a small personal note, a leaf from my own book, as it were: There I knelt in my bed one day, about six weeks after my heart attack, making love to my wife....And I want you to know, ladies and gentlemen, that despite all the talk and theory, despite all the research and the statistics and the cool nifty bits of advice, I want you to know that yours truly, El Professor here, was scared absolutely shitless."

Yes, that would be useful and informative. It was always a good idea to include a personal anecdote in a lecture.

It had been a pretty good lecture, actually. An important subject. Because doctors could be (and usually were) grossly negligent in these ways, doctors could make sexual cripples out of their patients—not just cardiacs: people with mastectomies, colostomies, other body mutilations, living silently with God knows what agonizing urgencies and anxieties—cripple them for good, simply by saying nothing. Or by saying the wrong thing, which could be even worse. Just before his own heart attack a man had come into the office, impotent, not knowing why. They soon found out. He'd had a coronary. In time he had found himself waking up with erections and with the nice old fevers, but he had been too scared to do anything. Finally, at the end of an office visit, he had asked his internist, "Is it safe to have sex?"

"Perfectly safe," the doctor had said.

"Are you sure?"

"Oh, absolutely. And if I'm wrong"—here the doctor had leaned way back in his swivel chair, folded his hands behind his head and laughed—"and if I'm wrong, what a way to go!"

From that moment, impotent.

So an informed doctor could make a powerful difference. He had been glad for the opportunity to give this lecture, and physicians always had listened to him with respect, since he was an expert, after all; and he had always spoken with confidence and authority, since he knew what he was talking about, after all.

Except that he hadn't known bugger-all. Not about the fear. None of his expertise had prepared him for the fact that the fear went this deep, choking desire out like a weed.

And then, kneeling there, wondering what might happen to him before this act was done, he had a sudden astonishing thought. Astonishing in that he had never discussed it as a doctor, he had never heard any other doctor discuss it, he had never even thought of it before. It was: Jesus! What about *her* fear?

Why had it never occurred to him to talk to the doctors about this? Of course, quite possibly, it would have occurred to women doctors.

I had so wanted this. It was a symbol, reassuring beyond all medical reports, reassuring beyond description. I hadn't anticipated that I would be so scared.

It seemed crucial that he not know how scared I was. Lying there silently, as though my mind were on my pleasure. Watching him in the half-light that came from the bathroom, seeing the fingers pressed so slyly against his carotid artery, wondering what the pressure told him. Feeling his rhythm, the contact so sweet, and hearing him breathe heavily like that, and wondering if it was okay or too much. Then feeling his body go still. Was he all right? Did I dare ask?

I felt poised at the edge of an irredeemable mistake. It would be dreadful to make him feel like an invalid here, of all places, in the bed. One wrong word and I might ruin it, erection gone, impulse gone, confidence gone, goodbye, and maybe for good.

And yet it might be even more dangerous to say nothing. For his body was in motion again now, and what if he was feeling pain, denying it, pushing himself to perform?

"Do you want to rest a moment?" I whispered.

Wrong. He made a sound like a sob and fell away from me, and we lay silent, not touching in any way.

Tell Me, Tell Me
Irving Kenneth Zola

Now I was the one who was nervous. Here we were alone in her room thousands of miles from my home.

"Well, my personal care attendant is gone, so it will all be up to you," she said sort of puckishly," Don't look so worried! I'll tell you what to do."

This was a real turn-about. It was usually me who reassured my partner. Me who, after putting aside my cane, and removing all the clothes that masked my brace, my corset, my scars, my thinness, my body. Me who'd say, "Well, now you see 'the real me.'" How often I'd said that, I thought to myself. Saying it in a way that hid my basic fear—that this real me might not be so nice to look at...might not be up to 'the task' before me.

She must have seen something on my face, for she continued to reassure me, "Don't be afraid." And as she turned her wheelchair toward me she smiled at me that smile that first hooked me a few hours before. "Well," she continued, "first we have to empty my bag." And with that brief introduction we approached the bathroom.

Anger quickly replaced fear as I realized she could get her wheelchair into the doorway but not through it.

"Okay, take one of those cans," she said pointing to an empty Sprite, "and empty my bag into it."

Though I'd done that many times before it wasn't so easy this time. I quite simply couldn't reach her leg from a sitting position on the toilet and she couldn't raise her foot toward me. So down to the floor I lowered myself and sat at her feet. Rolling up her trouser leg I fumbled awkwardly with the clip sealing the tube. I looked up at her and she laughed, "It won't break and neither will I."

I got it open and her urine poured into the can. Suddenly I felt a quiver in my stomach. The smell was more overpowering than I'd expected. But I was too embarrassed to say anything. Emptying the contents into the toilet I turned to her again as she backed out. "What should I do with the can?" I asked.

"Wash it out," she answered as if it were a silly question. "We try to recycle everything around here."

Proud of our first accomplishment we headed back into the room. "Now comes the fun part. . .getting me into the bed." For a few minutes we looked for the essential piece of equipment—the transfer board. I laughed silently to myself. I seemed to always be misplacing my cane—that constant reminder of my own physical dependency. Maybe for her it was the transfer board.

When we found it leaning against the radiator I reached down to pick it up and almost toppled over from its weight. Hell of a way to start, I thought to myself. If I can't lift this, how am I going to deal with her? More carefully this time, I reached down and swung it onto the bed.

She parallel parked her wheelchair next to the bed, grinned, and pointed to the side arm. I'd been this route before, so I leaned over and dismantled it. Then with her patient instructions I began to shift her. The board had to be placed with the wider part on the bed and the narrower section slipped under her. This would eventually allow me to slip her across. But I could do little without losing my own balance. So I laid down on the mattress and shoved the transfer board under her. First one foot and then the other I lifted toward me till she was at about a 45 degree angle in her wheelchair. I was huffing but she sat in a sort of bemused silence. Then came the scary part. Planting myself as firmly as I could behind her, I leaned forward, slipped my arms under hers and around her chest and then with one heave hefted her onto the bed. She landed safely with her head on the pillow, and I joined her wearily for a moment's rest. For this I should have gone into training, I smiled silently. And again, she must have understood as she opened her eyes even wider to look at me. What beautiful eyes she has, I thought, a brightness heightened by her very dark thick eyebrows.

"You're blushing again," she said.

"How can you tell that it's not from exhaustion?" I countered.

"By your eyes. . .because they're twinkling."

I leaned over and kissed her again. But more mutual appreciation would have to wait, there was still work to be done.

The immediate task was to plug her wheelchair into the portable recharger. This would have been an easy task for anyone except the technical idiot that I am.

"Be careful," she said. "If you attach the wrong cables you might shock yourself."

I laughed. A shock from this battery would be small compared to what I've already been through.

But even this attaching was not so easy. I couldn't read the instructions clearly, so down to the floor I sank once more.

After several tentative explorations, I could see the gauge registering a positive charge. I let out a little cheer.

She turned her head toward me and looked down as I lay stretched out momentarily on the floor, "Now the real fun part," she teased. "You have to undress me."

"Ah, but for this," I said in my most rakish tones, "we'll have to get closer together." My graceful quip was, however, not matched by any graceful motion. For I had to crawl on the floor until I could find a chair onto which I could hold and push myself to a standing position.

As I finally climbed onto the bed, I said, "Is this trip really necessary?" I don't know what I intended by that remark but we both laughed. And as we did and came closer, we kissed, first gently and then with increasing force until we said almost simultaneously, "We'd better get undressed."

"Where should I start?" I asked.

My own question struck me as funny. It was still another reversal. It was something I'd never asked a woman. But on those rare occasions on which I'd let someone undress me, it was often their first question.

"Wherever you like," she said in what seemed like a coquettish tone.

I thought it would be best to do the toughest first, so I began with her shoes and socks. These were easy enough but not so her slacks. Since she could not raise herself, I alternated between pulling, tugging, and occasionally lifting. Slowly over her hips, I was able to slip her slacks down from her waist. By now I was sweating as much from anxiety as exertion. I was concerned I'd be too rough and maybe hurt her but most of all I was afraid that I might inadvertently pull out her catheter. At least in this anxiety I was not alone. But with her en-

couragement we again persevered. Slacks, under-
pants, corset all came off in not so rapid succession.

At this point a different kind of awkwardness struck
me. There was something about my being fully clothed
and her not that bothered me. I was her lover, not her
personal care attendant. And so I asked if she minded
if I took off my clothes before continuing.

I explained in a half-truth that it would make it easier
for me to get around now 'without all my equipment.'
"Fine with me," she answered and again we touched,
kissed and lay for a moment in each other's arms.

Pushing myself to a sitting position I removed my
own shirt, trousers, shoes, brace, corset, bandages,
undershorts until I was comfortably nude. The comfort
lasted but a moment. Now I was embarrassed. I realized that she was in a position to look upon my not so
beautiful body. My usual defensive sarcasm about 'the
real me' began somewhere back in my brain but this
time it never reached my lips. "Now what?" was the
best I could come up with.

"Now my top...and quickly. I'm roasting in all
these clothes."

I didn't know if she was serious or just kidding but
quickness was not in the cards. With little room at the
head of the bed, I simply could not pull them off as I
had the rest of her clothes.

"Can you sit up?" I asked.

"Not without help."

"What about once you're up?"

"Not then either...not unless I lean on you."

This time I felt ingenious. I locked my legs around
the corner of the bed and then grabbing both her arms I
yanked her to a sitting position. She made it but I
didn't. And I found her sort of on top of me, such a
tangle of bodies we could only laugh. Finally, I managed

to push her and myself upright. I placed her arms around my neck. And then, after the usual tangles of hair, earrings and protestations that I was trying to smother her, I managed to pull both her sweater and blouse over her head. By now I was no longer being neat, and with an apology threw her garments toward the nearest chair. Naturally I missed...but neither of us seemed to care. The bra was the final piece to go and with the last unhooking we both plopped once more to the mattress.

For a moment we just lay there but as I reached across to touch her, she pulled her head back mockingly, "We're not through yet."

"You must be kidding!" I said, hoping that my tone was not as harsh as it sounded.

"I still need my booties and my night bag."

"What are they for?" I asked out of genuine curiosity.

"Well my booties—those big rubber things on the table—keep my heels from rubbing and getting irritated and the night bag...well that's so we won't have to worry about my urinating during the night."

The booties I easily affixed, the night bag was another matter. Again it was more my awkwardness than the complexity of the task. First, I removed the day bag, now emptied, but still strapped around her leg and replaced it with the bigger night one. Careful not to dislodge the catheter I had to find a place lower than the bed to attach it so gravity would do the rest. Finally, the formal work was done. The words of my own thoughts bothered me for I realized that there was part of me that feared what "work" might still be ahead.

She was not the first disabled woman I'd ever slept with but she was, as she had said earlier, "more physically dependent that I look." And she was. As I prepared to settle down beside her, I recalled watching her earlier in the evening over dinner. Except for the fact that she needed her steak cut and her cigarette lit, I wasn't particularly conscious of any dependence. In fact quite the contrary, for I'd been attracted in the first place to her liveliness, her movements, her way of tilting her head and raising her eyebrows. But now it was different. This long process of undressing reinforced her physical dependency.

But before I lay down again, she interrupted my associations. "You'll have to move me. I don't feel centered. And as I reached over to move her legs, I let myself fully absorb her nakedness. Lying there she somehow seemed bigger. Maybe it was the lack of muscle-tone if that's the word—but her body seemed somehow flattened out. Her thighs and legs and her breasts, the latter no longer firmly held by her bra, flapped to her side. I felt guilty a moment for even letting myself feel anything. I was as anxious as hell but with no wish to flee. I'm sure my face told it all. For with her eyes she reached out to me and with her words gently reassured me once again, "Don't be afraid."

And so as I lay beside her we began our loving. I was awkward at first, I didn't know what to do with my hands. And so I asked. In a way it was no different than with any other woman. In recent years, I often find myself asking where and how they like to be touched. To my questions she replied, "My neck...my face...especially my ears...." And as I drew close she swung her arms around my neck and clasped me in a suprisingly strong grip.

"Tighter, tighter, hold me tighter," she laughed again. "I'm not fragile....I won't break."

And so I did. And as we moved I found myself

naturally touching other parts of her body. When I realized this I pulled back quickly, "I don't know what you can feel."

"Nothing really in the rest of my body."

"What about your breasts," I asked rather uncomfortably.

"Not much...though I can feel your hands there when you press."

And so I did. And all went well until she told me to bite and squeeze harder, then I began to shake. Feeling the quiver in my arm, she again reassured me. So slowly and haltingly where she led, I followed.

I don't know how long we continued kissing and fondling, but as I lay buried in her neck, I felt the heels of her hands digging into my back and her voice whispering, "tell me...tell me."

Suddenly I got scared again. Tell her what? Do I have to say that I love her...? Oh my God. And I pretended for a moment not to hear.

"Tell me...tell me," she said again as she pulled me tighter. With a deep breath, I meekly answered, "Tell you what?"

"Tell me what you're doing," she said softly, "so I can visualize it." With her reply I breathed a sigh of relief. And a narrative voyage over her body began; I kissed, fondled, carressed every part I could reach. Once I looked up and I saw her with her head relaxed, eyes closed, smiling.

It was only when we stopped that I realized I was unerect. In a way my penis was echoing my own thoughts. I had no need to thrust, to fuck, to quite simply go where I couldn't be felt.

She again intercepted my own thoughts—"Move up, please put my hands on you," and as I did I felt a rush through my body. She drew me toward her again until her lips were on my chest and gently she began to suckle me as I had her a few minutes before. And so the hours passed, ears, mouths, eyes, tongues inside one another.

And every once in a while she would quiver in a way which seemed orgasmic. As I thrust my tongue as deep as I could in her ear, her head would begin to shake, her neck would stretch out and then her whole upper body would release with a sigh.

Finally, at some time well past one we looked exhaustedly at one another. "Time for sleep," she yawned, "but there is one more task—an easy one. I'm cold and dry so I need some hot water."

"Hot water!" I said rather incredulously.

"Yup, I drink it straight. It's my one vice."

And as she sipped the drink through a long straw, I closed my eyes and curled myself around the pillow. My drifting off was quickly stopped as she asked rather archly, "You mean you're going to wrap yourself around that rather than me?"

I was about to explain that I rarely slept curled around anyone and certainly not vice-versa but I thought better of it, saying only, Well, I might not be able to last this way all night."

"Neither might I," she countered. "My arm might also get tired."

We pretended to look at each other angrily but it didn't work. So we came closer again, hugged and curled up as closely as we could, with my head cradled in her arm and my leg draped across her.

And much to my surprise I fell quickly asleep—unafraid, unsmothered, and more importantly rested, cared for, and loved.

A Woman Dead in Her Forties
Adrienne Rich

Your breasts/ sliced-off   The scars
dimmed   as they would have to be
years later

All the women I grew up with are sitting
half-naked on rocks   in sun
we look at each other and
are not ashamed

and you too have taken off your blouse
but this was not what you wanted:

to show your scarred, deleted torso

I barely glance at you
as if my look could scald you
though I'm the one who loved you

I want to touch my fingers
to where your breasts had been
but we never did such things

You hadn't thought everyone
would look so perfect
unmutilated

you pull on
your blouse again: stern statement:

*There are things I will not share
with everyone*

2.
You send me back to share
my own scars   first of all
with myself

What did I hide from her
what have I denied her
what losses suffered

how in this ignorant body
did she hide

waiting for her release
till uncontrollable light began to pour

from every wound and suture
and all the sacred openings

3.
Wartime.   We sit on warm
weathered, softening grey boards

the ladder glimmers where you told me
the leeches swim

I smell the flame
of kerosene   the pine

boards where we sleep side by side
in narrow cots

the night-meadow exhaling
its darkness   calling

child into woman
child into woman
woman

4.
Most of our love from the age of nine
took the form of jokes and mute

loyalty: you fought a girl
who said she'd knock me down

we did each other's homework
wrote letters   kept in touch, untouching

lied about our lives: I wearing
the face of the proper marriage

you the face of the independent woman
We cleaved to each other across that space

fingering webs
of love and estrangement   till the day

the gynecologist touched your breast
and found a palpable hardness

3.
You played heroic, necessary
games with death

since in your neo-protestant tribe the void
was supposed not to exist

except as a fashionable concept
you had no traffic with

I wish you were here tonight   I want
to yell at you

Don't accept
Don't give in

But I would be meaning your brave
irreproachable life, you dean of women, or

your unfair, unfashionable, unforgivable
woman's death?

6.
You are every woman I ever loved
and disavowed

a bloody incandescent chord strung out
across years, tracts of space

How can I reconcile this passion
with our modesty

your calvinist heritage
my girlhood frozen into forms

how can I go on this mission
without you

you, who might have told me
everything you feel is true?

7.
Time after time in dreams you rise
reproachful

once from a wheelchair pushed by your father
across a lethal expressway

Of all my dead it's you
who come to me unfinished

You left me amber beads
strung with turquoise from an Egyptian grave

I wear them wondering
How am I true to you?

I'm half-afraid to write poetry
for you   who never read it much

and I'm left laboring
with the secrets and the silence

In plain language: I never told you how I loved you
we never talked at your deathbed of your death

8.
One autumn evening in a train
catching the diamond-flash of sunset

in puddles along the Hudson
I thought: *I understand*

life and death now, the choices
I didn't know your choice

or how by then you had no choice
how the body tells the truth in its rush of cells

Most of our love took the form
of mute loyalty

we never spoke at your deathbed of your death

but from here on
I want more crazy mourning, more howl, more keen-
ing

We stayed mute and disloyal
because we were afraid

I would have touched my fingers
to where your breasts had been
but we never did such things